ZACH

CYNTHIA WOOLF

Copyright © 2015 Cynthia Woolf

All rights reserved.

ISBN: 9781938887581
ISBN-13: 978-1-938887-58-1
ISBN-10: 1938887581

DEDICATION

For my wonderful husband, Jim. You support me and let me follow my dreams. Without you I couldn't do any of this. I love you more than words can say.

ACKNOWLEDGMENTS

Thank you to my critique partners Michele Callahan, Karen Docter, Jennifer Zane and Kally Jo Surbeck. You let me bounce ideas off of you and brainstorm with me when I write myself into a corner. I appreciate each of you so much.

Thank you also to my editor Linda Carroll-Bradd. My story is so much fuller, more rounded and just better with your help.

PROLOGUE

April 2, 1876
St. Louis, Missouri

The steel Zach Anderson pressed against his little brother's back was cold in Zach's hand. That he had to resort to this tactic to get Jake to come along irritated the hell out of him. The rain pouring out of the night sky didn't help matters.

"Knock on the door," demanded Zach, with a little poke of the gun barrel into Jake's back, angry and getting angrier by the minute.

Jake did as he was told and pounded on the front door, hard enough to be heard over the din of the rain.

"What the hell?" said his eldest brother,

Liam, when he opened the door. "Jake? Zach? What are you two doing here? It's the middle of the night."

"Are you letting us in or making us stand in this rain all night?" Zach growled from behind Jake.

Liam stood aside and let them in. "Zach, put away that gun."

"Can't until the kid is inside and we've talked to you."

Zach walked behind Jake into the foyer of the house his oldest brother owned in St. Louis. Both of them leaving puddles of water with each step.

Luggage and packed boxes lined the hallway down to the parlor.

"Sorry to do this to you, Liam. I know you're leaving tomorrow," said Zach.

"Yes. At first light. Before you get started, let me get you a couple of towels."

Liam left the room for a few minutes. Zach and Jake didn't say anything to each other. That's how it had been for the last twenty-four hours since they'd left Blackwater, Missouri.

Liam returned with two towels. "Now, *tell* me what's going on and why you brought Jake here at gun point."

Liam stood there in his nightshirt, robe and slippers, yet Zach didn't think they'd awakened his tall brother. Even with his boots on Liam and Jake both were four inches taller than Zach's own six feet. Both of his brothers were plenty strong, with lean muscles, Zach was just not as lean as they were. Liam was too alert to have been asleep.

"Only way I could get him to come." Zach rubbed the towel over his wet head. He saw Jake to the same

"And?" Liam ran his hand over his jaw. "Don't make me beat it out of you word by word, little brother. Just tell me the problem."

Jake and Zach dripped water from their coats onto the hardwood floor. *The rugs must already be packed.* "Sorry about the mess," said Zach. He took off his coat and hat and threw them on top of one of the trunks.

Jake followed suit, his blond hair dripping about his shoulders. He rubbed it vigorously with his towel.

They followed Liam into the parlor. Zach could still see Mary's feminine touches in the parlor even though she'd been gone for two years now.

Liam pointed at the two chairs in front of

the fire, then went to the fireplace, and stoked the banked coals to life. He added a piece of wood to the tiny flames before he turned once again to face his brothers. "Jake. You first," said Liam.

Zach winced hearing that familiar tone that allowed no leeway.

"I killed an army captain," said Jake. Gripping the back of the chair he remained standing.

"Why'd you do a damn fool thing like that?" asked Liam.

Jake shrugged. "I didn't have a choice."

"There's always a choice," insisted Liam, running his hands through his short brown hair, making it stand on end.

Zach put away his gun, sat and held his frozen hands out to the fire. He watched Liam's gesture, running their hands through their hair when they were frustrated was something all three brothers did. "No, there's not," said Zach. "There was reason for it, but he did kill the man. I use the word 'man' loosely."

"Damn it, Jake. They'll hunt you down and hang you for this." Liam was a colonel with seventeen years service. He knew about military justice.

"The son of a bitch deserved to die. And as soon as I can I'm going to kill the other bastard, too."

"He's mine," snarled Zach, clamping his jaw down.

"Who?"

"The colonel," said Zach.

"Jesus! You two had better tell me what's going on. Now. Start at the beginning."

Jake began to pace. He swallowed hard and took a deep breath.

Zach tracked his brother's movement knowing he didn't want to relive that moment when he lost Elizabeth, but he also knew Jake had to. For Liam. So he'd understand.

"I went to see Elizabeth. I'd go over everyday just to snatch a few moments together." His voice broke and he paused before gathering himself and starting again. "Her mother and aunt kept her pretty busy with wedding plans so it was hard for us to see much of each other.

"When I got there I heard a gunshot come from the house. I ran to the front door but it was locked and I had to break it down. I lost precious moments doing that. When I got to the parlor, two men were standing over Elizabeth. Her face was bloodied and her dress ripped, the skirt bunched around her waist. The one holding the gun was a colonel and the other was Longworth, a captain. Both in full uniform. The bastard captain was buttoning his pants when I walked in. I shot him on the spot." Jake stopped. His body shook, his hands were fisted and white knuckled.

"As soon as the colonel saw me he ran out the other door toward the kitchen. I followed but he was on his horse and riding away by the time I reached the back door."

He took several deep breaths to quell his tears before he could continue.

Zach looked at Liam and saw his eyes filled with pity. Zach felt the same way but he knew Jake had to finish, even if his voice sounded as though he was reciting a story. Zach figured it was the only way he could get through the retelling.

"I got back to the parlor and saw the captain was dead. I went immediately to Elizabeth and got down on my knees beside her. The bastard colonel shot her in the chest. She was still breathing. She opened her eyes. They were filled with terror until she realized who I was." His voice cracked and he tipped up his head to stare at the ceiling.

Zach knew that the memory was too fresh and painful. Blood pounded through his veins as rage filled him on Jake's behalf.

"She said to me: Jake, I tried to stop them, I tried. And I told her: Shh, you'll be fine. It's all right. With tears running down her cheek, she told me: I tried…tried to stop them…to stop John, but…and her last words were a whisper when she said: I love you, Jake."

Zach couldn't imagine what he was feeling. This had to be so hard on him.

Jake squared his stance to face Liam. "She closed her eyes and took her last breath in my arms. I held her for I don't know how long. Finally, I picked her up and laid her on the sofa. I went back to the dead captain and looked through his pockets to find out anything I could about the colonel."

"After he'd kicked the shit out of him," interjected Zach.

"The captain was John Longworth. His papers said he was stationed at Fort Leavenworth. Elizabeth was engaged to him before we fell in love," said Jake.

Liam turned to Zach. "Isn't that where

you're assigned?"

"It was," responded Zach, gritting his teeth.

"Was?"

Liam cocked his eyebrow in that way, Zach knew meant *explain*.

"Let the kid finish his story. Then, I'll get to mine."

Liam nodded. "Continue, Jake."

"I didn't know what to do, but I thought getting the sheriff was the right thing to do. I explained what I saw and what I did. Then I went to Mayor Green's office and told him. He sent someone to Aunt May's to fetch Elizabeth's mother. I didn't want Mrs. Green to come home and find the mess and Elizabeth…" He closed his eyes, hung his head and slowly took a deep breath.

"After that I went back to the house. The undertaker had already collected the bodies on the sheriff's order. With Elizabeth gone, there wasn't any reason to stay at the house, so I walked and walked."

He was pacing back and forth, like he was still walking after the murder.

"I walked all night and somehow ended up at home. The sheriff came out yesterday morning, brought my horse and took my statement again. That's when I found out there was another version of what happened. The bastard that got away was Richard Jordan. He told her father that I'd raped and killed Elizabeth in a fit of drunken rage and then shot his captain when he tried to stop me. Luckily, for me the sheriff didn't believe him, because I'd gone to him right away and he knew I wasn't drunk and wasn't raging against anyone but the bastards that did it."

His baby brother slumped into a chair; his legs apparently no longer supported him after reliving the whole bloody mess again.

"That's where I come in," said Zach. "The colonel was visiting the fort. Turned out Longworth was an old friend of his. Colonel Jordan ordered me and my men to go with him to arrest Jake. He is determined to see Jake hang to protect his career and his own neck. He wants Jake to be tried for murder in an army court. The long and the short of it is—I cold-cocked the colonel, my men looked the other way and I grabbed Jake and ran. Now we're both here and on the run from the law. I'll be court-martialed for attacking an officer and for desertion. Jake will be tried for the murder." Zach clenched his jaw, knowing his career was over. He wouldn't change it though. If he had it to do over again, he'd still take Jake and run. He was worth more than any career.

"Shit!" Liam turned his back on his brothers and stared into the flames that crackled and snapped. "Why'd you come here?"

"I knew you were leaving tomorrow. I wanted to see you before we disappear completely." Zach watched his oldest brother pace the carpet as Jake had been doing only minutes before.

Liam rested his hand on Jake's shoulder. "What about the sheriff and Mayor Green? Don't they believe you?"

Jake sat back in the chair and rubbed a hand over his face.

Zach knew he hadn't slept since it happened. He had to be exhausted, his nerves raw.

"As I said, the sheriff does believe me and didn't arrest me. Mayor Green knows Richard Jordan better than he does me. At least he thinks he does, Jordan being a friend of her ex-fiancé and all. He has the mayor convinced he and the captain came upon me and I shot the captain." He ran a hand around the back of his neck. "Mayor Green never did cotton to Elizabeth marrying me, a simple farmer, when she could have been a captain's wife."

Liam must have seen how tired they were.

"I know you'd like nothing better than to rest, but we leave now. Start packing the wagon. We need to make as much distance as we can before we stop tomorrow. It's going to be a long journey."

Jake sat forward in his chair. "Where are we going?"

Zach didn't much care where they went. Except for his family, everything that mattered in his life was gone.

"Deadwood. In the Dakota territory," said Liam. "I bought a claim."

CHAPTER 1

Thursday, June 28, 1877

Zach reined to a stop in front of the Deadwood mercantile. He was looking forward to seeing Lily, but more importantly, Lily had a spare room and he needed someplace to live. Hopefully, she'd be willing to rent to him.

He probably should get a bath and a shave before he talked to her, but he was just too dog-tired. Over the past three weeks, he'd chased Jordan to Cheyenne and then southwest toward Denver. Always behind him perhaps only minutes, but still behind. Only getting close enough once in Cheyenne, to have seen him.

Jordan could have killed him then, but Zach had seen him at the last moment and avoided most of the intended damage. The knife only cut him from below his eye to his mouth. It could have slashed his throat. Bleeding like a stuck pig afterwards, Zach had to find a doctor and get stitched up.

By then, he'd lost Jordan and didn't find him again until just outside Deadwood. Jordan was returning to Zach's home. Returning to the scene of his crime, when he stabbed Ellie, returning to finish what he'd started but Zach would not allow him to hurt his family.

The problem was finding him in the throng of people that now occupied Deadwood. Thousands of people had come and more were on their way. Looking for the same kind of riches that he and his brothers had been lucky enough to find. They'd struck the mother lode with the gold claim that Lily Sutter had sold them.

He should go next door and get cleaned up, especially if he hoped to have any chance of convincing Lily about the room. She wouldn't want a boarder who was as dirty as he was. He would ask her for meals, too. He needed them and sharing a meal, spending time together at her table, would be a good chance to get to know more about her and

Gemma. The little girl needed a father but until the threat that Jordan presented was eliminated, until *Jordan* was eliminated, he couldn't think about that. Couldn't think about a family of his own.

He and his brothers had been in Deadwood for ten months, nearly a year before he left to go after Jordan and he'd been trying to court Lily all that time to no avail. She was having none of it. In all his thirty-eight years, he'd never been turned down by a woman. But she said he was a Yankee and too handsome for his own good and wouldn't have more than a passing friendship with him.

Well, he wasn't too handsome now, not with the scar on his face from Jordan's knife. Red and angry, the wound still had the stitches. He needed to see Doc Cochran to get them out, today if possible, after he'd bathed. Then he could get a shave afterward and there wouldn't be any stitches left for the razor to catch on.

He dismounted and tied the horse's reins to the hitching rail then noticed a new bathhouse next door to Lily's store. The sign said 'Bath, shave and haircut' five dollars. He went in there first. The old man, Richardson, was there working.

"Good day, Richardson. I'd like a bath now and a shave later."

"You can do the bath but you have to pay Miss Lily," he said, the few strands of long gray hair combed over the bald patch on top, though not covering it very well. "And then bring the token back here. She's the one who does the shaves and haircuts since Sam left. You have to come back later for that, after she closes the store."

"Alright, let's just do the bath. Good and hot. I'll go get the token. I haven't had a good bath in weeks and am looking forward to this."

Zach walked next door to the mercantile. The bell sounded as he entered. The one customer in the store took one look at Zach, and left hurriedly, keeping her face turned and her hand over her mouth as she passed.

"Be right with ya'll," said Lily.

He walked up to the counter. "No hurry," said Zach, his voice still gravelly from lack of use.

Lily's head snapped up and she stared. "Zach. Is that you?"

"In the flesh."

She came around the counter. "You're

injured." Reaching up toward the jagged cut on his face, she pressed her lips together, a gentleness crossed her features before she rallied and the starch came back. "You're a mess. Where have you been? Why didn't you say goodbye?"

"Enough time for questions later. I need a bath and Richardson said I need to pay you. Here's the five dollars." He handed her a "half eagle" gold piece.

"All right, I won't bother you now. Here's your token."

"Thanks." He turned on his heel and left. When he got to the door he turned, as he always did, to see if she watched. He released a pent up breath, gratified that she was, tipped his hat and walked out the door.

~*~

Lily Sutter watched his retreating form as he walked out her front door, unbelieving the man she just saw was really Zach Anderson. The rugged, dirty man in worn buckskins was unlike any side of Zach he'd ever shown. He definitely wasn't the pretty boy, she'd thought him to be. Not with his face covered in scraggly beard and the jagged cut, new and still full of stitches that ran from his eye to just above his lip. It would affect his smile.

She'd always loved his cocky smile. But the man she just met didn't seem to know the word, smile. No laughter twinkled in his eyes, as there had been only a month ago. Now all she saw was hard resolve. She wasn't sure she liked the change in him. She knew how to handle the other Zach, she didn't know about this one. What had happened to Zach to make him the somber, serious man who had stood before her, asking for a bath? Where did the playful, fun loving person go?

~*~

Zach was done washing his body and his hair and stood in the tub. "Richardson, pour that bucket of water over me, please."

"Yes, sir, Mr. Anderson." The old man responded as quickly as he could, grabbing another bucket from next to the roaring fireplace and climbing on the stool next to the tub, he lifted it as high as his stooped shoulders would let him.

He poured the hot water over Zach, rinsing away all the dirt and grime from the last three and a half weeks. The water couldn't rinse away the memories of a trip that seemed a lot longer. Hard days in the saddle, being so close to Jordan he could smell him, then finally cornering him in an alley in Cheyenne, only to meet Jordan's knife with his face. Yet, all that encounter did was make Zach more determined to take care of this vermin, before he could hurt Zach's family.

Liam couldn't do it. He was newly married and had two children to think of, as well. Jake was no different—he had a new baby and a new wife. Both his brothers had wives, kids...*families* that Zach didn't. There was no one to worry about Zach. He was the only one who could stop Jordan. Stop the evil son-of-a-bitch before he killed the only people in Zach's life that cared about him, or that he cared for.

Zach dressed with care in the cleanest clothes he had in his saddle bag. He'd have to go to Liam's and pick up his clothes, but first he needed to ask Lily about the room. Angling his body to see himself in the broken piece of mirror, he combed his hair straight back from his forehead, then put on his hat. He'd needed a haircut before he left town; now his hair nearly reached his shoulders and curled on the ends.

His hat was covered in dust, but there

wasn't much he could do about it. He'd had Richardson brush his hat and coat while he'd bathed but they were both still the worse for wear. Rain and blowing dirt had ground the soil into them, and it wasn't coming out anytime soon.

He combed his mustache and beard, smoothing the curly black hair as best he could. Taking a last look in the mirror, he decided he'd done as much as possible to make the best impression on Lily. He wasn't the same man that left here a few weeks ago. That man was gone, in his place was a hardened version. A version determined to protect his family by whatever means necessary. He *would* kill Jordan, the event was just a matter of when.

Zach walked next door to the mercantile and stepped inside. Lily was waiting on a customer, and Zach killed the time by collecting supplies to restock his saddlebags. He wanted to be ready to leave at a moment's notice, if he needed to. He picked up hardtack, jerky and tobacco. He'd also have to get a bag of coffee. His supply ran out a week ago and he sorely missed it.

He put his purchases on the counter and

went over to the potbellied stove where the coffeepot sat. A shelf holding several cups hung above the stove. He grabbed one and poured himself some of the fragrant brew. As he took the first sip, he closed his eyes and let it slide down his throat, relieving dryness from the trip.

The bell above the door sounded and he turned to watch the customer leave. Now the store was quiet with just him and Lily.

"Zach. Are you ready to talk now?" She grabbed her coffee cup from under the counter where she kept it when there was a customer in the store. She walked over to the stove and filled the cup with fresh coffee.

He wasn't, but he couldn't avoid it any longer. "Sure. I guess you know why I left. I had to. I couldn't let him get away."

"Did you find him? Is it over now?" she asked with a pinched mouth.

"No." He didn't want to admit he's failed, not to her, not to Lily. "He's back in Deadwood and he knows about the family. I've a proposal for you."

She cocked her head. "We've been through this. I'm not marrying you... or anyone."

"Not that kind of proposal," growled Zach,

angry she still wouldn't consider marrying him. Well, that's alright, she'd change her mind; it was just a matter of time. He was a patient man regarding Lily. She was worth his patience.

Jordan wasn't. He would put everything he could into finding Jordan among the throng of unwashed that teemed the streets of Deadwood.

"I want to rent your brother's room. I can't go home. Liam and Eleanor are newlyweds, and they don't need me hanging around. Jake and Becky just had their baby and need time together without big brother getting in the way. What do you say? Before you answer, you know I need to protect you. Jordan knows about you, about us."

She gently shook her head. "There is no us," she whispered.

"You may think that, and it may be true, but our situation won't matter to Jordan. He knows I care about you."

"How could he know that? No one knows."

"Everyone knows except you it would seem." Irritated she still didn't believe he cared, he pressed on. "That's fine, you don't have to. I want you to think about what I've said. I'll be back in a little while and later when you close up the store, I need a shave and a haircut. I understand you are doing those now. Why?" concern flashed through him. "Why would you take on more when you barely had enough time to take care of you and Gemma, as it was?"

He watched her bottom lip start to quiver.

Ah, hell, she was going to cry.

She closed her eyes and gathered herself together. "I had a man working for me, Sam Toliver." Her voice quivered. "He was a barber, but also a miner. He managed the bath house and did the haircuts and shaves. I had him watch the store sometimes because I thought I could trust him. One day, I had to go to the hardware store and go get some bread from Mrs. Frederickson. When I got back, the store was empty and so was my strong box." She swallowed hard. "Three thousand dollars. Money I needed to pay Al Swearengen for my land."

He was by her side in two long strides. "Honey, I'm so sorry." He took her into his arms and, much to his surprise, she let him and it was like she always belonged there. "Why did you have that much money lying around?"

She buried her face in his chest and cried quietly, for a few moments. Then as if she'd remembered where she was and who she was with, she backed away from him.

He regretted the loss of her warm body next to his. She'd felt so right in his arms.

Leaning against the counter, she wiped her eyes then wrapped her arms around herself. "We don't have a bank and I don't have a safe. I was going to put it in the safe at the hardware store, but by then the money had already been stolen. I'm sorry. I didn't mean to cry all over you. I haven't had anyone to talk to." She sniffled and took a handkerchief from her sleeve. "If I do this, let you rent my room I mean, you have to do something for me. Something in addition to paying the rent."

Zach narrowed his eyes. "What do you have in mind?"

She dabbed at her eyes with the cloth. "I want you to get my money back. Sam has a claim up on City Creek and I doubt he's spent all the funds on liquor and whores. Before he does, I want you to get it back. There's no law here. The sheriff is useless. Unless you're Al Swearengen or one of his cronies, he has no to do anything."

He paused as though he was thinking about it. As if she even had to ask. He'd get back her money and this Sam person would rue the day he dared to steal from Lily Sutter. Zach would make sure of that.

"Okay, I'll do what you ask, but I want you to throw in meals and I'll help you out in the store again while I'm looking for Jordan. It should help you give you a little time to be with Gemma."

"Done."

The bell above the door sounded.

"Come back after the store closes, and I'll give you that shave and haircut. Then you can move your things into Horace's old room."

"You do realize the arrangement may start some tongues wagging... my boarding here."

She rolled her eyes at him. "Do you really think after all this time, that I really care what these people, or anyone for that matter, think of me?"

"No, I don't suppose you do. You couldn't and still have provided for Gemma like you have. You're a good mother, Lily." He gazed at her face and couldn't help but notice how blue her eyes were.

She blushed and waved a dismissive hand. He knew she wasn't as hard as she appeared, but after all she'd been through, she needed that extra coat of armor she'd acquired.

"I've got to see Doc about getting out these stitches, then you can give me that shave."

"That's fine. I won't be going anywhere." As if to reiterate that point, the bell sounded and another customer walked in.

Lily smiled, patted her hair and turned toward the door. "Hi there. What can I help y'all with today?" she said as she walked toward the newcomer.

CHAPTER 2

Zach made his way to Doc Cochran's at the other end of town. He walked up to the small, two-room cabin and knocked on the door, then pushed it open.

"Doc, you here?" he asked as he walked in.

"What do you want?" came the groggy voice from the back of the far room where the Doc's bed was.

He must have woken the man. "Sorry, Doc, I need to get out some stitches."

"Come back later. I've had a long night and need sleep now. I'll be here this afternoon."

"Sure thing, Doc. See you later."

Zach walked back out into the sunshine. The doc's cabin was always gloomy. There wasn't much light to begin with, the windows were small and invariably dirty, most of the light was provided by kerosene lamps. Zach was glad to be back into the warmth of the day.

He walked quickly back to the mercantile and collected his horse from in front of the bath house. Richardson sat outside the building, watching, making sure no one took Zach's horse, even though he hadn't ask him to.

"Thanks for watching out for me, Richardson," said Zach, flipping him a five dollar half eagle gold piece.

"Anytime, Mr. Anderson." Richardson snatched the gold piece out of the air. "Thanks."

Zach mounted, rode out of town toward Lead, and up Deadwood Creek. The dead trees, from whence Deadwood was named, had started to come back and the rocks gave way to the river on his left. Liam and Eleanor lived on the claim. Zach used to live there too, but not anymore. Someday he'd build a house in town for him, Lily and Gemma, but he had to convince Lily to marry him first. She looked to be as stubborn about it as she had been before he left. Maybe more so, since he hadn't explained to her before he left that he would be back. She probably thought he was leaving her like her ex-fiancé had when he'd found out she was pregnant.

He'd ridden for thirty minutes before he reached the cabin. Their gold mine wasn't too far out of town.

Liam had started to build onto the cabin to make it bigger. He wanted a place for lots of children. Eleanor was outside, wearing an apron to keep her pink skirt clean, kneeling in the front garden that Jake's wife, Becky, had originally put in. Her brown hair shined in the sunlight.

"Hi, Eleanor," said Zach from atop his horse as he pulled to a stop. He tied the reins around the hitching rail and went to give his newest sister-in-law a hug.

"Zach," squealed Eleanor. She rose quickly and opened her arms to him.

"How are you feeling? Are you healed?" he asked gently.

She smiled. It lit up her face, her eyes crinkled and a slight dimple appeared on the right side of her face.

That brilliant smile Liam told him about but, until she walked down the aisle on her wedding day, Zach had never seen.

"Better than you are." She gently touched her fingertips to his cheek and the wound there.

"Looks worse than it is. I went to get out the stitches, but Doc was sleeping."

"Come inside, I can take out those for you. I've done it before many times."

Zach followed her inside and looked at the cabin. They'd made some changes. The new stove Becky ordered stood against the far wall and provided a break between the kitchen and the living room. A pump was installed on the sink so Eleanor didn't have to go outside to get water anymore.

He noticed a pot of coffee and a tea kettle on the stove.

"Got any coffee in that pot?" He nodded his head toward the pot on the stove, then headed to the kitchen and a cup of the hopefully hot drink. He hadn't realized just how much he missed the stuff until after the couple of sips he'd had at Lily's.

"Sure do. I can make you tea, if you prefer."

He cocked an eyebrow in her direction.

"That's right. None of you Anderson boys

like tea. Although, I'm getting Liam to come around, I think."

"Come around? What am I coming around to?" asked Liam as he walked in the door brushing hay off his pants. From the looks of him, he'd been mucking the horse stalls in the new barn.

"Liking tea." She raised her cheek toward him for a kiss.

He grabbed her around the waist and kissed her soundly. Liam was tall, taller than Zach by a good couple of inches, but Eleanor was tall too, so he didn't have to bend much to kiss her lips.

"Liam. We have a guest," she said, color rapidly rising from her collar clear up to her forehead.

"No, we don't. It's Zach."

Proof that Zach was right in his decision to rent from Lily. He couldn't come back here to live, not with them acting like newlyweds. They needed time. Especially since Eleanor had been stabbed, they were still getting to know each other.

"Don't worry. I'm not here to stay. I just came to get my clothes."

"Of course, you're staying," said Eleanor.

She waved her hand toward his bedroom. "This is your home."

"No, it's Liam and your home. Mine isn't built yet and I think I'm building it in town."

"Where will you live in the mean time?" asked Liam.

"At Lily's. I'm renting her brother's room."

"Enough pleasantries." Liam crossed his arms over his chest. "Did you find him? Is he dead?"

Zach didn't mind the abrupt change of subject. He was surprised Liam hadn't asked him when he first came into the house.

"I tracked him back here. He's returned to finish the job. We all have to be on our guard."

"Where did you get that?" asked Liam, nodding in the direction of Zach's wounded face.

"Jordan. I had him cornered in an alley in Cheyenne. At least I thought I did. He surprised me and nearly sliced my throat, catching my face instead. Eleanor here, said she could remove the stitches."

"I can. Let me get my scissors."

She left the room.

As soon as she was gone, Liam closed in and was directly in his face.

"How could you let him come back here?"

Zach was prepared for his brother's angry reaction and he didn't take it personally. He knew Liam was scared for Eleanor, and for his children. Zach didn't want to tell him, but he was scared, too. Jordan was dangerous.

"I didn't have any choice. I lost him after he attacked me. I had to go to the doctor and get this stitched." He gestured toward his face. "By the time I got back to where he attacked me, I looked but his trail was already cold. I caught it west of Cheyenne and then lost it again until just outside of Deadwood. He's here, Liam, and there's not a thing I can do about that. But we are forewarned now. We can be prepared."

Liam ran a hand through his hair and nodded.

"Of course, we'll be prepared," said Eleanor, entering the room carrying her sewing kit. "I won't be surprised again and we'll protect the children at all costs."

"Eleanor," said Liam, and she went into his arms.

"I'm sorry, Ellie. Sorry he got away from me," said Zach. She was recovering from the stab wound where Jordan stabbed her, but that didn't make Zach feel any less guilt for not catching him.

"Don't be silly. We'll just have to make sure you get him here and take extra precautions until you do. I have faith in you. Now sit and we'll take care of those stitches."

He was glad she has confidence in him. Wish he did. He sat at the table and turned up his face to her.

She snipped and tugged.

"There. All out."

"Thanks."

She frowned and shook her finger at him. "Just don't make a habit of it. That's enough marring of your good looks."

"Lily always thought me a 'pretty boy'. Guess she can't say that now can she?"

"This did nothing to destroy the goodness on the inside Zach. She'll see that one day, if she hasn't already." Eleanor assured him.

"I should get my things and go. Lily will be closing the store soon and she's giving me a shave and a haircut."

"Good. You need one," said Liam

"She told me what happened…with her former employee stealing her money. I offered to give her the money she needed to pay off

Swearengen, but she wouldn't take it," said Eleanor, shaking her head.

Liam nodded. "More pride in that little bit of a woman than is good for her."

"No matter," said Zach. "I'm getting her money back. I'll be visiting the saloon tonight and if I don't find this Sam character there, I'll see him at his digs tomorrow." His body was stiff and his fists clenched. "Either way, he'll be repaying Lily what he took. All of it."

After visiting with Liam's family and making sure to see the kids, Zach gathered his belongings and made his way back to the mercantile by way of the livery. At least for tonight, he'd board his horse. When he saw Jake tomorrow he'd ask if he could keep the big chestnut stallion at Jake's for the time being.

From the livery, it was a short walk to the mercantile. He entered just as Lily was finishing counting her till.

"Have a good day?" He walked forward, only stopping because the counter separated them for the moment. He couldn't seem to get enough of her. He wanted her image, just as she was now, burned into his mind forever. Lily in a pale yellow dress, with white lace at the collar—all of which had seen better days. Her hair pulled back with small tendrils escaping the confinement and curling around her beautiful face. And her pouty pink lips, perfect for kisses. His kisses.

He still hadn't kissed her, but he would. When he got her money back, he was sure he'd get a kiss, maybe even two.

"Yes, we had a good day. Let's go over to the bathhouse and get you that shave and haircut. I hardly recognize you under all that fur."

Lily grinned.

He hardly recognized her. Such a beauty. It seemed it had been forever since he'd seen that smile.

"What about Gemma? It's kind of late. Do you want to feed her supper and put her to bed first?"

Frowning, Lily consulted her pin watch. "You're right. It's seven o'clock all ready. That last customer stayed a long time deciding which pants to buy the denim, the wool, or the duck. He finally decided on the denim. I told him we'd been hearing great things about how well they wear."

He leaned over the counter and placed his

fingers on her lips. "You're rambling, Lily. Let's go see Gemma, and you can show me where to put this bag." Flashing a smile, he lifted it so she could see that he did indeed carry a valise.

"Of course. Come with me."

After locking the front doors, she led the way through the back storeroom and up the stairs to the living quarters, to her home.

The rooms above the store were spacious. The parlor area, which was the first room off the landing, held a divan and two overstuffed arm chairs. In front of the divan was a low, coffee table. A higher table stood between the two chairs. A book rested on the high table next to a kerosene lamp.

The open area encompassing the parlor also held the kitchen and dining room. Lily's kitchen was simple. A cook stove, sink with a pump for water, and cupboards above and below the sink. To the right of the sink was a counter with more cupboards, and to the left of the sink was a small icebox.

In between the kitchen and the sitting area stood a rectangular table and four straight-backed chairs. Nothing fancy about any of it, but it was the most welcoming sight Zach had seen in months. Maybe even since before they'd left St. Louis to come to Deadwood. He got a pinch in his throat. He'd come home.

"This way to your room."

She led him down a hall to the first door on the left, opened it and stepped through.

"I know it's not much—"

"It's perfect," he said before she could finish. "Perfect."

A double bed, centered against the far wall, the headboard under a window, was covered with a quilt and two pillows in embroidered cases. Next to the bed, instead of a night stand, was a commode with a pitcher, basin, and kerosene lamp. A tall dresser stood against the wall, next to the door and a wardrobe beside it.

"Mama," said Gemma from the doorway.

He turned toward her.

Gemma stood there in a blue dress with white collar and cuffs. Her curly blond hair had been tamed into braids on either side of her head.

"Zach!" She ran to him, braids bouncing, and threw her arms around his waist.

He bent and gathered her into his arms, lifting her, hugging her like he'd never let her go. He'd missed her so much. Missed her little girl scent. It amazed him how this little bit of blond haired, blue-eyed fluff and her mother had gotten under his skin and into his heart.

"Hey there, sweet girl." He kissed her forehead and continued to hold her, her arms wrapped around his neck. It appeared she missed him, too.

Lily smiled at them. "Gemma, let Zach go so he can put away his things."

"Things away?" She cupped his cheeks with her little hands. "Zach are you stayin' with us?"

"Yes, sweet. I'm staying here for a while. Will you like that?"

She nodded. "I want you to stay here forever."

Zach looked over the top of Gemma's head at Lily.

He spotted her chewing her bottom lip, probably wondering if this was such a good idea. As soon as she saw Zach looking at her, she schooled her features.

"Zach will only be staying with us for a while, baby."

"Why?"

"Because, Zach will have his own place to

live before long and his business will have been taken care of. Isn't that right, Zach?" said Lily. She narrowed her gaze as a signal to support what she said.

He smiled at her. "We'll have to see." He wasn't telling her, he planned on living with her forever. On making her his wife and claiming Gemma for his daughter. If he told Lily that, she'd hightail and run. Already, he'd worn her down some, because she wouldn't have considered renting the room to him six months ago. But he'd worked with her, gotten to know her and she'd gotten to know him. She learned he wasn't just another Yankee, but a good man who had nothing to do with the destruction of her home.

He wasn't the man he used to be. He'd probably been no better than her ex-fiance, love 'em and leave 'em was his philosophy. Until Lily. She'd changed him, just by being herself.

Zach set Gemma on the floor. "Let me put away my clothes, then we'll play something before supper, while your mama cooks."

"Her mama, doesn't have to cook. Supper's been cooking all day. Stew. Venison stew. Hope you don't mind it," said Lily.

"No, I like it just fine, and I'm sure I'll like yours best." He turned to Gemma. "Do you have any checkers for after dinner?"

"I don't know," she shrugged. "Mama, do we have any checkers?"

"Yes, in one of the kitchen cupboards. I keep meaning to teach her to play but there is never enough time. Gemma, you come with me and leave Zach alone for a little bit. You can help me by setting the table."

Gemma nodded and walked to her mother, then turned back to Zach. "I'm glad you're here."

"So am I, sweetheart." He grinned. She was only one of his sweethearts, her mother was the other, unbeknownst to her.

Gemma skipped out of the room and turned toward the parlor.

"I'll leave you to unpack. I've got that stew for supper when you're ready, along with some good bread from Mrs. Frederickson. I'm getting Gemma started now. She always takes a long time to eat because she's so excited to tell everything she did during the day. I'm sure she'll keep us both entertained." She turned and hurried out of the room.

Zach smiled. He made her nervous…well,

being in the bedroom with him made her nervous. She was attracted to him more than she would admit, and she couldn't hide that. He saw her gaze dart from him to the bed and back again, before she looked away.

She was also scared. He understood that. She'd been grievously wounded by her ex-fiancé, so Zach would have to prove, he wasn't the same kind of man. That he'd stay, no matter what. Before he could do more than kiss her hand or maybe her cheek, he'd have to keep his distance and earn her trust.

CHAPTER 3

Dinner was more boisterous than he would have imagined.

Gemma talked nearly the entire time, except when her mother reminded her to eat. She was so excited to have Zach there.

He was almost as excited as she was. It was nice to have a child at the table again. He missed Liam's kids, David and Hannah. She was almost the same age as Gemma and just as talkative. Gemma was another reason he felt so at home.

Afterward, Lily found the checkers and Zach played with Gemma while Lily cleaned the dishes. When she was done, she came over and watched the match proceed.

"You didn't eat much."

Patting his full stomach, he laughed. "I ate

two bowls. That's plenty. I got out of the habit of eating until I was full while on the trail. Hard to feel full on hard tack and jerky."

"After I put Gemma to bed, I'd like to hear about your trip."

He looked across the little table at this strong woman, then reached out and put his hand atop hers. The difference was shocking. His dark-tanned hand and her porcelain-white one. The contrast between them, as people, was almost as stark. He was a Yankee, had been a Union soldier during the War between the States. She was a Southern belle whose home had been burned by Yankee soldiers.

In some ways, she still saw the soldier, not the man. He never let his men do what had happened to Lily but he knew other officers had. Some had even joined in on defiling every female on the plantation before burning it to the ground.

With a shake of his head, he brought himself back to the present. "Not much to tell, but I'll tell you whatever you want to know. I have no secrets from you, Lily."

She cocked her head to the side. "Everyone has secrets, Zach. We have to in order to survive in this world."

"I don't. Not from you." He gave her hand a little squeeze. "Maybe from other people but not from you. Never from you."

She lowered her head.

But he could see she didn't believe him. He'd prove it to her, answer anything. He loved Lily, she just needed to relax her guard and lower that armor, to realize she loved him back. If she didn't, she would never have let him move in here with her and Gemma.

Zach missed a play and Gemma won the match.

"Yay! I won! I won!" She jumped up and down shouting.

"Yes, you did, sweetheart. Time for bed," said Lily as she stood.

"Will you really be here in the mornin'?" said Gemma to Zach.

"Yes, darlin', I will be here in the morning. You and I will have our breakfast together with your mama before she and I go work in her store."

He looked up at Lily, where she stood next to the table and saw her smiling.

"What?"

"You said *her* store."

"It is *your* store. It will always be *your*

store. You've put the blood, sweat and tears into this place to make it a going concern. No one can take away that achievement."

She looked down at the floor, "You could have said 'the store' but you didn't. You acknowledged that it's mine." She looked at him and smiled brilliantly.

"I don't understand what you're getting at, but if it makes you happy, then I'm all for it. I love seeing that smile on your face."

She blushed and looked down at her feet.

He was reminded of Gemma's reaction to being complimented. It was the same. Neither one seemed to realize how special they were.

"Shall we get you that shave and haircut now?" said Lily, turning away from the sink where she'd set the dishes to soak.

"Sure, if you're ready."

"Let me tuck in Gemma and then we can go to the bath house," she said to Zach.

She came back a few minutes later.

"She wants you to say goodnight."

"Okay, be right back."

He went into Gemma's room which was across the hall from his. Painted pink, it was definitely a little girl's room. He wondered if his niece, Hannah, would have her room painted that color, too. Although maybe by now it was. He'd forgotten that when he left, David and Hannah were still sleeping in the living room. Now that he wasn't living there, they could each have a room. He'd have to make sure Liam knew he wasn't moving back. No matter what happened with Lily, the time had come for him to find his own place to live.

"Zach?"

"Yes, sweetheart, what can I do for you?"

"Stay, Zach. Don't leave."

"I'll stay as long as your mama will let me."

"Good. I think Mama likes you a lot."

"What makes you say that?"

"'Cause she's always smilin'."

"Is that so?" Her declaration made his heart beat a little faster.

"Yup.

"Good to know. Now goodnight, Pumpkin."

"Goodnight, Zach."

He came back to the parlor after kissing Gemma goodnight. Lily was sitting in one of the dark brown overstuffed chairs, reading by the kerosene lamp. She looked so comfortable, he didn't want to make her leave it.

"Do you want to do this tomorrow?" he asked softly. "You look like you could use some quiet time right now."

"No, it's alright." She closed the book, with a piece of paper inside to mark her place, and then set the book on the table between the chairs. "Now is as good a time as any."

"If you're sure."

She nodded. "I am. Are you sure you trust me to cut your hair and shave you?"

"More than anyone else," he assured her.

She cocked her head and shook it a little. "You're a strange man, Zach Anderson."

He grinned at her. "And you're a wonderful, gracious woman, Lily Sutter."

He loved making her blush like she was doing right now. He probably should stop it. The woman was a perpetual shade of pink since he'd gotten here, but he couldn't help it. He meant every compliment. She was special and she needed to know how much.

She took a deep breath, "Zach, you've got to stop saying those things."

He shrugged. "Why? They're true. You need to know how truly wonderful you are. You take yourself too much for granted, Lily."

"I don't. I just do what I need to do."

"And that makes you an amazing woman. Lots of people, men and women alike, would have given up by now or taken the easy way out. You didn't, and I can't see you ever giving up."

Lily put the book down and rose from the chair. "Let's go get this done. And stop saying nice things to me or I just might have to slit your throat."

He grinned. "You wouldn't do that. You like me, even if you don't admit it."

"Fine," she said, rolling her eyes. "I do like you, but I still won't marry you, so you can get that thought right out of your head."

"Never. I'm determined, but I won't harass you about it. I want you to get to know me and know that I mean what I say. I'm not him and I'm not like him. I need for you to believe it deep inside."

"You ask a lot of me, Zach. Too much, I think. I don't know that I'll ever believe that just because you're nice now, you won't leave if you get what you want."

How could she think so little of herself? "What I want is for you to marry me. I'm not leaving, and I'm not asking that you take me to your bed before we marry." His voice rising and his muscles tensing, he said, "I'm *not* him, Lily."

"We'll see." She nodded, dismissing him and the subject. "Let's get your hair cut before it gets too late. Let me get a plate of food for Richardson. He's a good man, even if a little unreliable."

He took a couple of deep breaths and regained his calmness. "Ready when you are."

They walked downstairs and out of the store to the bath house and barber shop. Lily had a chair set up for shaves and haircuts. Three straight backed, wooden chairs formed a row against the wall for waiting customers .

Richardson sat in one of those while he waited for bath customers. He also slept in the room behind the bathing room as part of his pay, and kept the water hot until midnight for those miners who came to town late.

She gave him the plate of food.

"Thank ye, Mizz Sutter, ma'am." He took the meal, put his coffee cup on the floor and began to shovel the food in.

Zach shook his head. The man must have been hungry.

"Richardson, do you know Sam Toliver? The man that used to work here?" Zach removed his buckskin coat and put it on the back of one of the wooden chairs.

He swallowed the food in his mouth before speaking. "Oh, yes, sir."

"Is there anything about him that I could use to recognize him?"

"Yes, sir. He's got this fancy, red feather in his hat. You can't miss it."

"Thanks. That's exactly what I needed to know."

He raised his eyebrows. "You gonna get Mizz Sutter's money back?"

"I am."

"Good luck to you. She's a good lady." He looked around, cautiously, "Be careful. Sam don't fight fair, so don't give him a chance."

"Thanks for the tip. I won't."

Lily took the soap cup and spun the shaving brush around inside until a good lather formed.

"Wet your face from the water in the basin, please."

This was an unusual request but he complied.

"It helps to soften the beard and make it easier to cut," she said.

"I know." He cocked an eyebrow. "It may not look it right now, but I have done this a couple of times."

After drying his face, he sat in the chair. Lily had on its lowest setting so she could easily reach his face. She spread the lather on his beard, then took the straight razor and sharpened it on the leather strop, attached by one end to the wall. With careful strokes, she scraped away a swath of dark hair revealing skin whiter than the rest of his face.

His skin would get color again in no time but for a short time he would have two tones on his face.

She shaved him slowly, carefully, resharpening the razor after every three or four swipes down his face.

He ran his hand over his clean face. It was probably the best shave he'd ever had.

"I've done everything except your scar. I'll be very careful but you tell me if you feel anything you shouldn't."

He sat back again. "I'm not worried. Go ahead."

The scar was tender and the lather irritated it a little, but having her touch him, even though it was just a shave, felt too good to have her stop.

She ran her fingers over his face, checking

for spots she might have missed.

He hoped she found some so she'd have reason to keep touching him.

"Done," she pronounced. "Now the hair."

She combed her fingers though his hair, loosening it from where his hat tamped it down.

Zach had to stop himself from groaning with pleasure. She leaned in and he was faced with her breasts, close enough that if she was naked he could take one in his mouth. That had him salivating and caused a certain part of his anatomy to come to life. He smelled her rose soap, delicately scenting her skin. The thought of other men enjoying this part of the service crossed his mind and jealousy rose, unbidden, and it was all he could do to tamp it down and remind himself, this was Lily. His sweet Lily. He needed to find another barber for this place and fast. Before that, he had to somehow make Lily understand, and see reason why she couldn't continue cutting hair.

"Um, Lily. Are you almost done?" he asked not trusting the tone of his voice.

"Yes, why?" She smoothed the last lock of his hair to the side and checked the length with her comb.

He got up from the barber chair and paced in the small space between the chair and the counter behind it. "I don't want to upset you, but I don't think you ought to do haircuts anymore."

"Why? You haven't even seen it yet." Her voice cracked a little.

Damn. He'd hurt her feelings.

"No, that's not it." He stopped pacing. "I'm sure the haircut is fine, great even. It's just that...when you're in front of me...leaning over...you're close enough for me to, um, take your breast in my mouth...if I wanted. And much as I would love to do just that, I don't think you want your customers thinking like that."

She burst out laughing and crossed her arms over her stomach.

What? Not exactly the reaction he'd been expecting.

"Well, that explains the big tips and why some of my customers are here every week or so for a trim."

He laughed with her. It was impossible not to, her laugh was infectious. "I guess you better find a male barber fast."

"I guess I better. You want the job?"

Frowning, he shook his head. "No, I can't cut hair worth beans."

"Just teasing. You want some coffee before bed?"

"Much as I would like that, I'm looking for this Sam character tonight. I figure I'll start at *The Gem* and work my way through the worst of the brothels. I doubt he's somewhere like *The Bella Union*. Probably too classy a place for the likes of him."

"Oh." She nodded and set the scissors on the counter behind the barber chair. "I hadn't realized you were starting so soon. I thought maybe you could relax tonight and get after him tomorrow. You've been on the road for a long time."

He looked at her, saw the loneliness there. "You know, you're right. Tomorrow would be better. I've been alone for quite a while and could use the company. That is, if you don't mind."

"No, I don't mind. In all honesty, I could use some adult conversation, too. Something that doesn't involve selling you a pair of pants or fifty pounds of flour."

A grin spread. "Let's go then. I'll tell you all about my trip."

~*~

Lily still couldn't believe she'd said yes to Zach's proposition. Even if she really did need the money, if she was going to pay off her loan with Swearengen and keep the store supplied.

But the boarder was Zach. The one man in the world who tempted her. Not because he was about the most handsome man she'd ever seen, but because he seemed to genuinely care for her and for Gemma. And Gemma adored him. She'd taken to him like no one else before or since. Maybe the reason was because he was with his little niece, Hannah, when they met, but Lily thought it had more to do with the man himself and how he was with Gemma. He cared for her and it showed.

Still, Lily held herself back. He was a Yankee, true, but most of all, she was just plain afraid. Afraid that if she let herself fall for him, if she let herself *love* him, she'd be bereft when he left her just like Beauregard had. She couldn't stand that, the desertion, the feeling she wasn't good enough. Not again. It had hurt, because she thought herself well and truly in love. Now, of course, she understood she'd been infatuated, and Beauregard had never intended to marry her. Later on, she discovered she wasn't the only woman he was *engaged* to that became pregnant, or that he deserted, hurting and alone to deal with the consequences of their indiscretion.

Putting that out of her mind for now, she got a cup of coffee for both of them, and they sat at the table where Zach proceeded to tell her about his trip.

"I chased Jordan from the cabin to Lead and on to Cheyenne. There I found him in a saloon. He escaped out the back to the alley and I followed. As soon as I cleared the door, I was attacked and Jordan slashed at me with his knife. I dodged out of the way and almost escaped unharmed, but the weapon caught me just below the eye. I was lucky it didn't take my eye." He sipped his coffee. "He ran, coward that he is, and I couldn't see well enough through the blood to hit him, when I fired my gun.

"I staggered back into the saloon, got a towel from one of the girls and the directions to the nearest doctor. The doc stitched me up and I backtracked to the saloon to pick up his trail—"

"Didn't you even rest for the night? My God, Zach, you'd just been wounded."

"There wasn't time. I had to get back on his trail before I lost it. Tracking someone in town is hard enough. As a matter of fact I thought I had lost him, but then I found his trail again outside of Cheyenne." He gritted his teeth. "That's when I discovered he was on his way back to Deadwood."

Lily refilled their coffee cups and got down a plate of molasses cookies from the high shelf in the cupboard.

"Don't tell Gemma. She'll eat the whole batch if she knows where I keep them. She has a terrible sweet tooth," she said, setting the plate on the table between them.

Zach grabbed one of the dark brown cookies and took a big bite. "These are great. I haven't had a fresh baked cookie in a long while."

Pleasure flashed through her at the compliment. "I'm glad you like them. I like to bake but the only chance I get is on Sundays after church and I usually have to use that time to do laundry and clean the house."

"See," said Zach. "That's another reason you need me. I can help you with the store so you can do those things during the week and have your Sundays to rest or bake or do whatever you want." He raised his eyebrows, "maybe even spend time with me."

It would be nice to be able to have someone to share the workload. "You're incorrigible."

"Proudly. I haven't changed my mind, Lily. If anything I'm more determined. While I was gone the ones I really missed were you and Gemma. Not my brothers, not their kids, but you. Don't get me wrong. I missed them but I missed you more. Thoughts of you two were the only things that kept me going sometimes."

"Don't say those things. Please don't." Her heart beat faster. She liked to hear them but she shouldn't.

"I'm sorry." He leaned back in his chair. "I don't mean to make you uncomfortable. Let's just put this behind us. I still intend to help you in the store, but beyond that, I won't push you."

She nodded. "Thank you."

They were silent for a few minutes. Neither one seemed to want to be the first to break the silence. Finally, Lily said, "Well, I suppose we should go to bed—"

Zach grinned.

"—I mean to sleep."

He laughed. "I know what you mean, but it was fun to watch you." He rose and took his coffee cup to the sink. "Goodnight, Lily."

"Goodnight, Zach."

She watched him walk down the hall to his room. His broad shoulders filled the space and she couldn't stop a shiver over her skin. She wondered again if this was such a good idea. Did she really need the money enough to put her heart at risk?

CHAPTER 4

The man entering the store swaggered. Actually swaggered. Zach had heard people, women especially, describe someone as swaggering, but he'd never witnessed it before. The man was shorter than Zach, wore a brown suit with a white shirt and brown tie. His hair was brown and his mustache and beard were brown. There was nothing much to make him stand out from the walls of the building around them.

He approached the counter.

"Where is Lily?" he demanded.

The man's tone nearly sent Zach over the top of the counter and at the man's throat, but he was on his best behavior. This was Lily's store and the man was one of her customers.

He needed to remember that. "Miss Sutter is indisposed right now. Can I help you?"

"No. I'm here to see Lily." The man looked down and examined his fingernails.

He was treating Zach like he was an insect too far beneath him for more than a cursory glance and Zach's jaw clamped shut and he ground his teeth. Who the hell did this man think he was? "Well, *Miss Sutter* won't be back for a while. Can I give her a message?"

"Yes, tell her Ralph was by and will see her on Sunday."

"Sunday?" repeated Zach, eyebrow raised.

"Yes, I'll pick her up at nine o'clock Sunday morning for church."

Zach said nothing, but fumed inside. Who the heck did this jackanape think he was? "I'll tell her."

Ralph turned on his heel without another word and left the store, the bell above the door signaling his exit.

"Who was that?" asked Lily, entering from the back room.

"Ralph," growled Zach. "He said he'd be by to pick you up at nine on Sunday."

Lily blushed and glanced away.

"Who the hell is Ralph?"

"He's a man that has been escorting Gemma and I to church. That's all."

"Well, it's not all to him. He seems to think you belong to him."

"He does not," frowned Lily.

"Yes, he does. Believe me, a man knows when another man has staked his claim. Surely, you knew that would happen if you let him escort you to church every Sunday." He scrubbed at the counter with the rag in his hand, not seeing what he was doing, but concentrating on Lily. She really didn't understand, and all Zach wanted to do was strangle this Ralph person.

"Well, I never," huffed Lily.

"Now that I'm back, I'll escort you to church or anywhere else you want to go. At least, I'm open and honest with you. I want to marry you and I don't care who knows it."

"Zach, I…" she looked away.

He lifted his hand. "Don't say anything, now. We'll just play it by ear and see where it takes us. Alright?"

She was quiet for a minute, but finally nodded.

Her response was all Zach could have asked for. He smiled.

ZACH

~*~

Zach came out of his bedroom on Sunday morning, and Lily nearly dropped her coffee cup when she saw him. He wore a black three-piece suit, with a perfectly tied cravat, a silk vest, watch fob and watch, and carrying what looked like a brand new black Stetson hat.

He looked as handsome as she'd ever seen him and he put Ralph Emerson to shame. She'd only let Ralph escort her because she knew nothing could ever come of the association and he kept away other men. At least he had…until Zach.

Zach would keep away other men with just a look in their direction.

She wore her best dark blue silk dress. The frock wasn't in the latest style, having been one she saved from the fire of her plantation twelve years ago, but it still fit and still flattered her skin and hair. The effect was grand and she always received compliments.

When Zach saw her, he whistled. "You look lovely."

She lowered her head, looking at the floor, and whispered, "Thank you."

Gemma sat on the couch, kicking her legs against the front of it. She wore a pale pink dress Lily had ordered through the Montgomery Ward catalog. It had white lace at the collar and cuffs, with a wide ruffle on the bottom of the skirt. She wore her lace-up boots which Lily had cleaned as best she could.

"Shall we go? Ralph will be waiting downstairs," said Lily.

Zach scowled. "I thought we discussed this. I'll be taking you to church from now on."

"Yes." She nodded her head. "We did. But I haven't told Ralph. I owe him that much."

They got downstairs and greeted Ralph, just as the stage from Cheyenne was pulling to a stop.

"Ralph, this is Zach Anderson, my new boarder."

Zach shot her a look—one she knew meant he was much more than just a boarder and wanted her to let Ralph know that. She ignored him.

"Boarder?" He looked Zach up and down. "That's not wise, Lily. What will people say?"

"In Deadwood?" she asked. "Nothing. And if they do…well, I don't much care for the good folks of Deadwood that would begrudge me from a source of income because of how the situation looks. Are you one of those people,

Ralph?"

"Uh, no, no, of course, not," he blustered, grabbed his coat by the lapel, puffed out his chest and squared his shoulders.

"Ralph? Is that you?" called a large, dark-haired woman, who'd just disembarked from the stage. She was flanked by four children, three strapping boys and a toddler girl.

"Harriet?" stammered Ralph. "What are you doing here?"

The woman walked over to them, carrying the little girl, followed by the boys, who appeared to be in age from mid teens to about seven or eight. The girl was about two.

"We've come to join you, of course. I wanted to surprise you, and it looks like I have."

Lily cocked an eyebrow at Ralph. "You never mentioned you were married, Ralph. How lovely that your family arrived in time for you to escort *them* to church."

He adjusted his tie and cleared his throat. "Huh? Oh, yes, yes, it is a wonderful surprise."

"Won't you introduce me to your friends, dear?" asked Harriet with a cock of her head toward Lily, Zach and Gemma.

"Of course, my dear. This is Lily Sutter, her

daughter Gemma, and Zach Anderson." He waved his arm toward his family. "My wife, Harriet, and my children, Ralph Junior, Ben, Joseph and Margaret.

Lily walked down the steps and held her hand out to Harriet Emerson. "Very nice to have you here. I bet you are not in the least bit interested in going to church right now and wish to have Ralph take you and your children to his home to freshen up."

"Uh, yes, my dear, this way." He picked up one of the trunks and his son, Ralph Junior, picked up the other.

"Very good to meet you Mrs. Emerson. I own the mercantile here." She pointed over her shoulder at the building behind her. "I'm sure we'll be seeing a lot of each other."

Ralph hurried off with his family in the direction of his home.

"Well, that was interesting," said Lily.

She looked over at Zach and burst out laughing. The look on his face was one of anger and disbelief at the same time.

Zach stood there for a few moments, staring after the retreating backs of Ralph and his family. "The old bastard. Married and trying to court you at the same time. Wonder if he has other families elsewhere?"

How awful. Lily sobered. "You really think he might have done this before? And perhaps been successful?"

"I don't know why not." He cocked an eyebrow. "He had you convinced, didn't he?"

She took a deep breath and focused on straightening her cuffs. "Zach, there was never anything between us, nor could there have been. He was just a way to keep other men at bay. I never wanted and would not have allowed anything more than the escort on Sunday's that he was providing." She stole a peek at his face.

His mouth was drawn into a tight line and he shook his head.

"I certainly never would have allowed him into my home."

At that, he nodded and put out his elbow toward her. "Shall we go?"

"Yes, please, can we go?" said Gemma.

She'd been such a good and quiet girl that Lily almost forgot she was there. Gemma hadn't said a word when Ralph showed up or when his family had. Come to think of it, she never talked to Ralph in the three weeks he'd been taking them to church, he'd never had a word directed his way from Gemma.

"Gemma, did you like Ralph...er...Mr. Emerson?"

She shook her head.

"Why?"

"He made me feel icky."

What did I miss? Was I so concerned with keeping other men at bay that I didn't care about how my daughter felt? "I see."

"Out of the mouths of babes," said Zach, with a smile down at Gemma.

Lily looked up at him, took his elbow with one of her hands, and tried to take Gemma's hand in her other.

Gemma ignored her, ran around and grabbed Zach's hand.

"So it would seem. I suppose I should pay more attention to my daughter. She seems to know quite a lot about people."

"That she does," said Zach, with a grin. "Shall we go?"

"Yes."

They walked toward the large tent at the west end of town.

~*~

They finished singing the last hymn and some folks were already preparing to leave when Eleanor Smith Anderson rose and approached the pulpit.

"Attention, everyone," she said. "I want to let you know that in three weeks, on Sunday, after services, there will be a box lunch social. All the ladies will bring a box lunch, and the gentlemen will bid for the privilege of having lunch with that lady. All the proceeds will go toward the building fund for the first permanent church building to be erected on the ground we stand on."

Everyone exchanged glances and started talking at once.

Eleanor raised her arms up and down, asking for silence. "There is one rule. Only the money you have with you can be used. No promise notes and no I.O.U.'s. Cash only. We will have scales on hand for any gold that is brought. So, men, start saving your money."

The entire congregation clapped.

Zach grinned at Lily. He knew he could out-bid anyone in the congregation for Lily's lunch basket.

"What are you grinning at? You eat with me every day. Why would you want to spend hard earned money, to buy my lunch at the social?"

"To send a message to every other man there."

Her brows lowered. "What message?"

"That you belong to me."

"Do I belong to you, too, Zach?" asked a small voice.

With a smile, he looked down at Gemma. "You bet you do, Sweet Pea. Both of you are my special ladies."

"Zach—" said Lily, shaking her head and letting out a long breath.

"I'm glad, Zach," said Gemma. "'Cause you belong to me, too."

She skipped away to join the other children playing outside the tent.

He waved a hand toward Gemma. "See, I belong to her and to you too, if you'll let me."

Lily turned away. "All I see is a little girl who will be hurt when you leave."

Zach placed his hands on Lily's shoulders and brought her gently back to rest against his chest. "I'm not going anywhere. You can't chase me away."

"I wish I could believe you," she said quietly, almost on a sob.

"You can. In your heart, you know you can."

She stepped away from him and he immediately missed her rose scent and missed her soft body.

"I can't think when you touch me."

He too stepped away, giving her the space she needed. "And I can't think of anything but touching you. But I won't. I want you to think. I want you to know that I'm different. I'm not him and I never will be. I won't leave you, Lily."

She jutted up her chin. "You already did. You left chasing that man and never told me you were going."

"We were different then. I was just the man that worked in your store so my niece could play with Gemma. The man that returned to you," he pointed to his chest. "The man I am now is the man who loves you and wants to marry you."

Her fist flew to her mouth on a sob.

"I'm sorry. This is no place to be talking about this. Let's go home. If you want to talk more, we can or we can just leave it be...for now."

After inhaling a long breath, she nodded and let him take her arm.

"Gemma," he called over his shoulder.

"We're going home now. Let's go."

CHAPTER 5

Zach spent what little time he could make himself take away from Lily, searching the local saloons for Sam Toliver. The thief. He stopped at *The Gem* first, as he usually did, and this time, he got lucky.

One of the men who worked at the Anderson Bros. Mining Company, pulled him aside when he came in.

"Hey there, Boss," said Harry Mills. "You still lookin' fer that Sam Toliver fella?"

"I am."

"That's him over there at the faro table." Harry jerked his chin toward a table surrounded by men playing a card game. "The one in the dirty buckskin coat with the bright red feather in his hat. Cocky bastard, he is.

Doesn't seem to care who knows he stole that Mizz Sutter's money."

"He'll feel differently in a few minutes, I guarantee," snarled Zach, his fists clenched in anticipation.

"I'll be here to back you up, Boss."

"Thanks. I appreciate it. Hope I won't need your help."

Zach walked over to the faro table, came up behind Sam and tapped him on the shoulder.

Sam turned and snarled. "Whadda ya want? Can't ya see I'm winning?"

"Glad to hear it. Now cash out. You're through."

"Who says?"

"Zach Anderson. I'm here to collect what you owe Lily Sutter. You see no one here may care that you stole her life savings, he scanned the area and most of the men raised their hands and backed away, but I do. Now cash out and hand over every penny you have or die right here and I'll take it anyway."

"I don't owe that bitch nothin'."

"Wrong answer," said Zach, as his fist connected with the other man's jaw and nose, knocking him to the floor.

Blood from his broken nose ran down his chin on to his shirt and he groaned.

"Try again," said Zach. Grabbing handfuls of buckskin, he pulled the man up to his feet, then he levered back his fist to hit him again, if he needed to.

"Okay, okay." Sam cashed out and handed over that money, plus what he had in his pockets, to Zach. "That's all what's left." He took a dirty rag from his back pocket and held it to his nose.

Zach counted it and his blood raced when he realized it was short. "There's only eighteen hundred dollars here. Where's the rest?"

"Gone. I spent it."

Beads of sweat rolled down Sam's temple into his beard. "Honest, Mr. Anderson, I don't got no more."

"Well, listen up. You're paying back every penny." Zach lifted a finger to Sam's face. "You're going to go back to work for Lily as a barber every evening. Every red cent you make doing that you're giving to Lily. Half of everything you pan on your claim will go to Lily. You bring it in every Saturday to be weighed.

He put his finger on Sam's chest and

pressed. "If you don't come in...if you try to run...I'll track you and you'll wish you'd never been born. Understand?"

Wide-eyed Sam nodded.

"Good." Zach pocketed the money and walked out of the saloon back to Lily's. *Back home.* He wanted to run to her but didn't want to frighten her so he consciously calmed himself.

When he got there, he saw Lily was waiting up for him, as she always did.

"Did you find him this time?" she asked, putting her book on the side table and rising from the chair where she'd been reading.

"I did." Pride filled him when he set the money, a mixture of bills, coins and a bag of flake, on the table.

Lily came up behind him and helped him off with his coat, then hung it on one of the pegs behind the door.

"Thank you," she whispered, her back still turned to him.

"Don't thank me yet. All he had left was a little more than eighteen hundred dollars."

Her gaze snapped to his. "Oh, God, that's not enough. The note is due and I owe Al Swearengen three thousand dollars." She held herself, arms wrapped around her waist.

Zach went to her and took her hands in his. "Let me give you the money."

"No. I can't do that." She shook her head. "I refuse to take money from you or anyone."

"Then let me loan you the money. What difference does it make if you owe me or him? It's still a loan and you can make payments, as you can. You won't have to worry about losing the store or becoming a prostitute for Swearengen. Better yet, let me be your business partner. A silent business partner. I'll provide whatever capital you need for a small percentage of the net proceeds of the business. What do you say?" *Please say yes, anything so I can stay close to you.*

She stared at him for what seemed like forever.

"You would do that for me? You wouldn't try to tell me how to run the business? You'd be a truly silent partner?"

"Truly. Not a word about how to run the business. Seems that you're doing rather well as it is. You don't need me coming in and messing with a good thing."

She started to cry, covering her face with her hands.

He wrapped her in his arms, knowing she'd agreed to let him help her. "Don't cry, honey. It's alright." She was wearing her nightgown and robe, the cotton soft beneath his fingers as he rubbed up and down her back in what he hoped was a soothing gesture.

She looked up, her pale blue eyes full of tears.

"Kiss me. Please, Zach, just kiss me."

She didn't need to ask twice. He lowered his head and took her soft lips with his. She tasted so good, like coffee and molasses cookies. He could taste her all night.

He tried to be gentle. But he needed her closer and clasped his arms around her, bringing her lush curves against him. His body responded immediately and his shaft became rock hard against her belly.

With reluctance, he broke the kiss. "Do you feel how much I want you? Marry me, Lily, so we can make love every night. So we can be together always. Marry me and put me out of my agony."

"You know I can't." She leaned back and put her hands on his chest. "I won't be put in the position to be hurt again. I can't go through that, and I won't put Gemma through that. I shouldn't even take the chance, having you live here."

"You need my protection. You know Jordan is still out there, waiting for any opportunity to kill everyone I love, including you. He stabbed and nearly killed Liam's wife Ellie. I'm not giving him the chance to do that to you." *The thought of her alone with Jordan on the loose make his blood run cold.* "Until we find the maniac who stabbed Ellie, you're in danger. Anyone Liam, Jake or I care about is in danger. Putting you in jeopardy is the only thing I'm sorry for. I'm not sorry nor will I apologize for loving you. Ever."

She pulled out of his arms. "Don't say that. Don't say you love me. You don't know me."

"I know everything I need to know. You're fiercely independent, you're loyal to your friends, you love your daughter, you're beautiful and you love me—"

She shook her head. "I don't."

"—even if you won't admit it."

"You're delusional. I needed the money." She crossed her arms over her chest. "That's why you live here. Now that you're loaning me the money, I should probably throw you out."

He grinned at the color rising in her cheeks. "But you won't. Admit it you like having me here. You like the conversation, the companionship, as much as I do. And it's good for Gemma. Let me tell you right now—no matter what happens between us, I will never abandon that little girl. She's mine as far as I'm concerned. And I suspect as far as she's concerned, too."

She smiled. "I'm glad you love Gemma. She needs you. Needs a man to look up to. Do you want some tea before bed?"

She changed the subject and he let her. There would be lots of opportunities later to change her mind and make her realize she loved him and needed him as much as he did her. And change it he would, even if it took a lifetime. Without Lily and Gemma, there was no life.

"Thanks, but I think I'll head to bed. I've got to start searching for Richard Jordan tomorrow, before he finds us. We're not hard to find because we're not trying to hide. He is." He points to the window, "Don't let Gemma go outside by herself, at least until we get him off the street."

"I won't. And…thank you for everything. I

don't want you to think I'm not grateful for what you've done. I truly am."

"You're welcome. Now I'll take my leave." He walked back to his bedroom, leaving her to think about their conversation. He hoped leaving her was the right thing to do.

Zach closed the door to his bedroom, sat in the wooden chair he'd brought in and toed off his boots. Next came his suit coat and vest which he hung in the wardrobe, followed by his pants and shirt which he laid over the back of the chair.

Lastly, he shed his drawers. He slept in the nude, not wanting to be restrained by clothes during sleep. He liked the feel of the cool sheets against his bare skin, even in the dead of winter. Admittedly, he'd much rather feel Lily's skin as he held her in his arms while they slept, after making sweet, tender love. But he'd have to wait for that dream. He was a patient man, but that didn't mean he wouldn't do everything in his power to change her mind.

~*~

Zach dressed for working in the store in a plain white shirt and black wool pants. His apron would cover most of the pants and save them from spilled flour or other staples. He'd help Lily out for a while and then go after Jordan.

He was up before Lily and made coffee, started the bacon and cut the bread to fry after the eggs were done.

Lily came out of her room, dressed in her robe and nightgown looking deliciously rumpled.

"Is that coffee I smell?"

"It is. You want some?"

"I'll get it. You're up awfully early," she said, getting a cup and filling it with the hot, black brew. She added two teaspoons of sugar and cream from the icebox, then took a sip. "Ah, just what I needed. I could hardly get out of bed this morning."

"Didn't you sleep well?"

"No," she admitted. "Tossed and turned all night."

"I'm sorry. I hope the cause wasn't our conversation last night."

"No," she answered quickly, "it was just one of those nights."

He turned back to the stove and the bacon sizzling in the skillet. "I'll open the store if you'd like to go back to bed."

"Thanks but the best thing for me is to get

to work."

Gemma walked out of her room, rubbing the sleep from her eyes.

"Good morning, sweetheart," said Zach.

"Mommy, I don't feel good."

Lily frowned. "Let me feel your forehead, baby." She got on her knees and touched Gemma's forehead with the inside of her wrist. "You're burning up. Let's get you back to the bedroom and into bed."

"What do you want me to do?" asked Zach. He knew about fevers and children. Liam had almost lost Hannah to the flu three years ago. Now with Gemma, fevers frightened him even more.

"Make me a bowl of ice water and get Doc Cochran."

"Sure thing." He took the bacon off the burner so it would stop cooking. Then he got the basin from under the sink and pumped water into it. He took the block of ice out of the top of the icebox, chipped off several good-sized chunks and put them in the basin.

Then he reached down a glass, filled it with water, took it and the basin back to Gemma's room.

"Here you go. I brought some water in

case she's thirsty. Last time I remember Hannah getting sick, we had to keep pouring liquids down her."

Eyebrows wrinkled, Lily nodded. "Thanks."

"I'll go get Doc Cochran now."

Lily nodded again without looking at him. She was rinsing a cloth in the cold water and laying it on Gemma's forehead.

About an hour later he returned with the doctor in tow.

"Let me see her," said Doc, putting his bag on the floor next to Gemma's bed.

Lily rose from the bed and came to stand next to Zach.

The doctor listened to Gemma's chest, checked her temperature with a thermometer, lifted her nightgown and examined her tummy.

"Lily, come here please," said Doc Cochran.

After glancing at Zach, she walked over to the bed.

"Do you see these spots on Gemma's chest and stomach? That is measles. She'll have to be isolated for about two weeks until the spots go away. If you nor Zach have had the measles, then you'll probably get them because they are contagious."

"I've had them," said Lily, brushing Gemma's hair away from her forhead.

"So have I, but what about the kids at the school?" asked Zach.

"Anyone around Gemma in the last two weeks has been exposed," said Doc, his gaze flicking between the adults. "All those children, the folks at church, anyone she came into contact with in the store. They've all been exposed and carried it home to their families. We'll have an epidemic in no time and there's not a thing we can do about it but ride it out."

"I've got to let my brothers know not to send the kids to school and to watch for symptoms. I don't know if Liam's kids have had the measles or not."

"Go," said Lily with a wave. "Warn them so Ellie can close the school for the time being."

He stepped close and wrapped her in his arms. "She'll be just fine. I've had them and survived. Gemma will, too." He kissed the top of her head, left the bedroom and grabbed his hat and coat from the pegs on the wall behind the front door. "I'll be back as quick as I can."

He rode to Jake's first, not knowing if

Hannah and David were there or not. He hated the thought that baby Jenny might have been exposed. She was so small, less than two months old.

Zach knocked on the door.

"Hi, brother. Come in, don't stand on the porch like a stranger."

"I can't. Are Hannah and David here?"

"No. They went home last night. Why?"

"Gemma's got the measles. You need to keep an eye on Jenny. She's been exposed, which doesn't mean she'll become ill, but she probably will. She'll get a red rash on her torso and face, it's very itchy so she'll be really uncomfortable. You might try cool oatmeal baths, because she'll have a fever, too. Just don't panic. Doc Cochran will be really busy, but have him come see you or take Jenny to him if you have to."

Jake's face filled with worry and Zach felt guilty for putting it there, but preparing him for what might happen was best.

Jake ran his hand through his hair.

It was a gesture Zach knew well because all of them, Liam included, did the same thing when they were frustrated or anxious.

"Thanks for coming by and warning us.

We'll make sure to watch Jenny for the symptoms."

"I'm headed to Liam's now to warn them. Eleanor's will have to close the school until this passes."

"That's not going to make any of them happy."

Jake stuck out his hand to shake his brothers.

Zach shook his head. "Don't think I should, but you know I love you. Give Becky and Jenny a kiss for me."

Jake nodded and slowly closed the door.

Zach rode up the river to their mining operation and Liam and Eleanor's home. He dismounted and wrapped the reins around the hitching rail in front of the house. He was about to knock on the door when it opened.

"What are you doing here so early? I thought you were at the store full-time now." Liam pulled up his suspenders as he stepped onto the porch. "Come on in and have a cup of coffee."

"Sorry, I can't come inside and I can't stay. I just came to warn you that the kids have been exposed to measles. Gemma came down with them this morning. Ellie will have to close the school until the outbreak passes."

Liam grimaced. "I'll let her know, but neither she nor the kids will be happy about this."

"Let her know what?" asked Ellie from behind Liam.

"Gemma has measles. You need to keep the kids home and close the school for a while. Doc figures we'll have an epidemic and there's not much we can do about it."

"Oh, dear," exclaimed Ellie, lifting a hand to her throat. "Those poor children, and their parents too, if they haven't had the measles before. I've had them so I'm not worried about me. I've worked in wards where outbreaks happened. The illness is miserable and can be a dangerous disease."

"I need to get back to Lily," said Zach jerking his thumb over his shoulder. "I'm going to open the store and run it so she can stay with Gemma."

"You're really in love with her, aren't you?" asked Liam.

"I am," confirmed Zach with a wide smile. "I've asked her to marry me more than once, she keeps turning me down. Maybe when she realizes I'm really here to stay, she'll trust me enough to say yes."

"I wish you luck. When we get over this outbreak, maybe you, Lily and Gemma could come for supper. You can bring us up to date on the search for Jordan."

"Nothing to bring up to date. I've been looking for Sam Toliver, the man who robbed Lily. I found him last night, but he was short on the money he stole. That reminds me. I need two thousand dollars right away. Can you bring the money to the store later today? I can't wait for it right now."

Liam nodded. "Sure thing. Should I ask what it's for?"

He hooked his thumbs through his suspenders and puffed out his chest with pride. "I've become a partner in Lily's store. She needs the money to pay off the land she bought from Al Swearengen. And I want to make sure I have enough money to outbid anyone at the box lunch social in a couple of weeks."

"Not taking the chance that she could have lunch with another man, huh?" laughed Ellie.

"No way. She's mine. She just refuses to acknowledge it. But I'll prove to her I've changed. I'm not like the man who left her. I'll never leave her, even if she throws me out, I'll still be there for her, whenever she needs me."

Ellie seemed surprised by his declaration.

"You're a good man, Zach. Lily knows that, but she's scared. She's been hurt badly in the past and doesn't want to go through that again."

"I know, Ellie. That's why I'm willing to wait for her, for as long as it takes, but that doesn't mean I'm standing by idle. I intend for her to know that I want her, I love her. I really have changed. I need to make her see that."

"She will, just give her time."

Zach nodded. "I've got to go. The store is supposed to open in half an hour. See you this afternoon."

He walked to his horse and mounted then turned and waved at Liam and Ellie, before kicking the horse into a gallop.

CHAPTER 6

When he arrived back at the mercantile, he had just enough time to check on Lily and Gemma before he opened the store. He went up the back stairs.

Doc had gone, and Lily was in Gemma's room.

"How is she?" asked Zach softly.

"Better. I've gotten her a little cooler, but she's started scratching and that's not good."

"Did the doc tell you about oatmeal baths? They'll help fight the itching. Try some witch hazel, too."

Lily rose from the chair next to Gemma's bed, walked to him, looked back at her baby, then quietly shut the door as they left the room.

"Doc mentioned the oatmeal, but not the witch hazel."

"They'll both help with the itching but she'll still be miserable."

"I know," she shuddered. "Even now I remember that horrible itching with both the measles and the chicken pox. But getting them now is better for her in the long run."

Zach agreed. "She'll be better in no time. I have to open the store now."

"Thanks, Zach…for everything."

Smiling, he said with a salute. "That's what partners are for."

He walked downstairs and unlocked the front door, turned over the open sign and put on a pot of coffee. Then he got his apron and began to sweep the floor in long, even strokes so as to keep the dust minimal. In less than fifteen minutes the bell over the door rang, signaling the first customer of the day.

Zach put the broom against the wall and walked back to the counter where the man waited.

"Good day, what can I do for you?"

The man was of average height, several inches shorter than Zach. He wore a dark gray three piece suit, with black cravat and a black bowler hat. All he needed was a cane to mark him a complete dandy. Zach tried not to smile.

"I'm looking for Lily Sutter," he said.

His southern accent so thick, he made Lily sound like a Yankee by comparison.

"She's unavailable. I can help you with anything here you might need."

"I don't need anything," he said curtly. "Except to see Lily."

"As I said, she's unavailable," Zach's muscles tensed and his hands drew into fists. As his temper started to rise, his voice grew softer. "I'll give her a message for you. Who can I say called?"

The man drummed his fingers on the counter, then said, "Tell her Beau Parkerson called. She knows who I am."

Zach was pretty sure he knew who this Parkerson was, too, and wanted to beat him into the ground for what he'd done to Lily. At the same time he was grateful to the man because if Parkerson hadn't abandoned Lily, then she wouldn't be here with Zach.

"I'll give her your message."

"I'll return tomorrow."

"As you wish. I can't guarantee she won't still be indisposed. As a matter of fact, I can almost guarantee that she will be unavailable, but you're welcome to return."

He turned on his heel and left, slamming the door behind him.

Apparently that wasn't what Beau wanted to hear.

Zach gave him a cocky smile and a salute to his retreating form.

Lily entered from the back storeroom. "My goodness, who was that? What were they so angry about?"

Zach wasn't sure he wanted to tell her, but she had a right to know. To be prepared to meet her ex-fiancé and put him in his place. Or Zach would. Beating the man to a bloody pulp would give him great pleasure.

"That was Beau Parkerson and he was looking for you."

"Oh, God. No." Her hand formed a fist and flew to her mouth. "It can't be."

She was whiter than the lace at the neck of her dark blue dress.

"Lily. I won't let him hurt you or Gemma. No matter what I will protect you."

"I know, but what if…if he wants to take Gemma from me?"

"No." His gut twisted into a knot. "He'll

have to go through me and my brothers first. This is Deadwood. Who will they believe, a stranger or several pillars of the town? Not to mention the richest men in the territory? And you…you're the owner of the only mercantile between here and Cheyenne." He cocked his head toward her. "Don't sell yourself short. You're an important member of the community."

She shook her head and began to pace. "I'm not. Some people look at me like I might as well be working at *The Gem*. What am I going to do?"

Zach stopped her by pulling her into his arms. "Whatever you decide, we'll do it together. Right now, we need to concentrate on getting Gemma well. How is she?"

Lily took a deep breath. "Better. She's sleeping. That's why I decided to come downstairs and see if you needed me."

"I always need you, just not to help with the store. For now, I can manage it on my own. You need to concentrate on Gemma. I'll put off Parkerson for a few days, until we see how the baby girl is doing, and until you've had a chance to decide what you want to do."

She stepped back and Zach let her go.

She clasped and then unclasped her hands. "I need to check on Gemma," she said as she turned and fled up the stairs.

The conversation was over. She was scared but of what? Her feelings for Zach? Or of Parkerson who had left her years ago, alone and pregnant. What could he want with her now? If Lily, didn't send the man packing maybe Zach would take matters in his own hands. Literally.

Two nights later, after supper, he and Lily sat in the parlor. Gemma was back in her bed having eaten some chicken broth. The spots were more prevalent and a few had shown up on her beautiful face. She was being such a good girl and not scratching them. Lily put socks on Gemma's hands at night to protect her, so she couldn't scratch in her sleep and open up the sores.

"I want to see him," Lily said without stopping her knitting.

Zach put down his book. "Why?" He'd been expecting the statement but his gut still clenched.

Without looking up from her knitting, she said, "I need to find out why he's here and get him moving along. I hope he's just chasing gold, but it's possible he's looking for me and Gemma, even though he doesn't know about her. He just knows I was pregnant when he left me."

"He's a bastard any way you look at it. Please just let me send him on his way." He punched his fist into his hand.

She finally looked up at him. "No. I won't let you demean yourself that way."

She rolled her neck.

Zach knew she was stiff and sore with worry and looking after Gemma. He rose and went behind her chair, and then he smoothed his palms down her neck and over her shoulders. His thumbs worked back and forth in small motions over the knots in her shoulders until they released and relaxed.

"I don't consider protecting you to be demeaning."

"Ahh, that feels so good." She hung her head down in front of her to give him access to the back of her neck. "You'll feel sorry if you beat him to a pulp."

"No, I won't. I assure you, sorry is not in my vocabulary where this *man* is concerned."

He rubbed a little harder.

"Oww."

"Sorry." He backed off and made his moves gentler. He couldn't let his feelings for the *bastard*, as he now thought of Parkerson, get out of hand while he was working on Lily's shoulders.

"No, I'm just so worried about Gemma," said Lily, putting her knitting in its basket.

He stopped massaging her and was hard pressed not to put a kiss on her shoulders where his hands had just been.

"Thank you. That felt wonderful."

"You're welcome." He sat in his chair. "And as to worrying about Gemma, you're her mother, it's your job to worry, but she's doing better. She's sleeping and eating, her fever has subsided. She's doing great."

"I know. So what's wrong with me? I should be happy."

"You're concerned about Parkerson. Let's meet him together. He'll be in tomorrow at ten." He leaned forward in his chair toward her. "It's always at ten. You'll be there too, and we'll see what he's up to."

She nodded. "Alright. I'm going to bed now. See you in the morning."

He wanted to kiss her good night but she wasn't ready for that. Seeing her already worried about tomorrow, he didn't want to give her anything else to be concerned with. He'd try to move slowly, but he'd be there if she needed him.

~*~

Lily paced back and forth behind the counter, looking at her pin watch every few seconds. At five after ten, she said, "Where is he? You said he's always here by ten."

Zach wasn't upset by her impatience. He understood it. She wanted to get this done and over with as soon as possible. He looked through the glass panes in the doors out into the thoroughfare and saw Parkerson crossing Main Street toward the mercantile. His jaw tightened.

"He's coming. Are you ready?"

She grabbed his hand and squeezed. "I'm ready as long as you're here beside me."

"Always."

The bell over the door sounded.

Zach moved behind the counter and stood next to Lily, his hand at her waist for support.

The *bastard* strutted up to the counter. Zach figured he didn't know any other way to walk. Cocksucker.

"Finally, I get to see you, Lily."

"What do you want, Beauregard? I have work to do."

Single eyebrow raised, he looked around at the store, currently empty of customers. "Yes, I can see you are overrun with people who want to buy things. And you know I prefer that you call me Beau."

Zach flinched at the sarcasm in his voice.

"No customers just means we can do the work needed to keep the customers coming back. So state your business and be gone."

Beauregard didn't spare a glance at Zach. "Lily, do you think we might converse somewhere private?"

She shook her head and crossed her arms over her chest. "This is a private as you get. Anything you want to say you can say in front of my fiancé and partner. Did I introduce you to Zach? No?" She gestured between the men and then wraps both arms around Zach's elbow. "Zach Anderson, this is Beauregard Parkerson. The bastard who left me alone and pregnant."

Zach's heart burst with joy, that she called him her fiancé, until he looked down at Lily, who was gripping his arm as if her life depended on it. Did it? Was she that afraid of this man?

"Now, Lily that was just a little misunderstanding."

"Beauregard," Zach held out his hand.

He took it gingerly.

Zach latched on and squeezed.

"Hey, that hurts," Beauregard said, pulling back his hand and rubbing it with his other.

"Sorry," said Zach with no remorse. "I owe you a debt. If you hadn't left Lily, I never would have found her. I'm pleased to say she's to be my wife."

"Very well, I came to see Lily when I heard she was here in town. I was hoping she might give me a…a grubstake. I believe that's the term. I want to try my hand at gold mining."

Lily laughed. "You? Do manual labor? I don't believe it. You have fallen low."

Beauregard reddened but straightened and gazed around the shop. "I have fallen on some hard times. You seem to be doing well; perhaps I should just stay here. After all you were to be my wife."

"I'm doing very well, no thanks to you. I've done this on my own and I'm proud of what I've accomplished."

"The emphasis is on the word *were*," said

Zach, eyes narrowed. He wasn't trying to look menacing, he *was* dangerous to this man and Parkerson needed to know it. "She's to be *my* wife now and I don't appreciate you thinking you can come here and have Lily support you. Take your leave before I put my fist through your face."

Beauregard backed up, looked down at the counter.

He seemed to think it provided him some modicum of safety.

"I'll leave when I feel like it. You can't tell me what to do. I'm here to see Lily not you."

Zach vaulted over the counter and took Beauregard by the lapels. "Is this really how you want this to end? I can let you walk out of here on your own two feet or throw you out. Lily?" he said, not taking his gaze off Beauregard.

"Yes, Zach," she answered sweetly.

"Would you open the door for this riff-raff?

"Certainly." She came around the counter and hurried to the door, pulling it wide open.

"Too late," said Zach. "You had your chance."

He hauled Beauregard to the door and

threw him out into the muddy, waste infested street.

He landed face first in a pile of horse dung.

Lily closed the door and turned.

Zach stood brushing off his hands on his apron, as though they had just handled some sort of filth.

She grinned, grabbed his head and brought it down to her. "Thank you for everything." She kissed him hard and fast.

Hardly giving him time to respond.

He wrapped his arms around her and, when she started to pull away, he shook his head. "This is the way it should be done." Slowly, with infinite care, he took her lips with his, slanting his mouth over hers. He rubbed his tongue along the seam of her lips and when she opened, he plunged in. He was gentle, yet he devoured her. He had waited so long. The time seemed like forever.

The door bell rang and they broke apart, having forgotten they were standing in front of the mercantile's entrance.

"Well," said Liam, "looks like you two will be the talk of the town. Do you have something to tell me?"

Zach grinned.

Lily blushed but said, "No. Nothing. Zach was just helping me out."

He thought he'd been making progress. He thought that Lily meant it when she said he was her fiancé, but she'd only been using him. Despite his best efforts, he was angry and fought to hide his feelings.

For the rest of the day, he and Lily didn't talk much about what happened. As a matter of fact, they didn't talk much. Period. Zach remained angry, and every time they were without customers, Lily blushed and said she needed to check on Gemma.

Finally, Zach had enough of her scurrying off whenever they had the chance to talk.

The last customer left, and Lily said, "Well I need to go check—"

"No."

"But…"

"Gemma is fine. Lily, we need to talk." He stood with his arms crossed over his chest. "Why did you tell him I'm your fiancé? You could have said friend or partner or any number of other things besides fiancé. You know how much I want to marry you. Why would you do that to me?" He hated the plaintive note that crept into his voice.

"Oh, Zach, I was scared. I thought if he wanted Gemma, who he still doesn't know about, that it would be better if he thought you were my fiancé." She held herself around the waist. "I never meant to hurt you."

"Why won't you marry me? I know that you love me."

"I don't." She shook her head. "I thought I was in love with Beauregard, too, and look how that turned out. I don't want to make the same mistake again."

"With us, it wouldn't be a mistake. We already live and work together, and we get on very well. At least I think so. What is it that is separating us?"

"I'm scared. I don't deny it. I'm scared right to my very toes. What if we're making a mistake? What if…"

"Shh." He put his fingers over her lips and gazed at her agitated face. "We won't talk more about it now. I've got some thinking to do and so do you. What do you really want out of life, Lily? Is this store and Gemma enough? Don't you want more children? A husband? A chance to travel and see the world? Is living here in Deadwood enough for you?"

He took off his apron and set it on the

counter. "I need to start tracking Jordan. Until I find him, we're stuck with this situation. I won't leave you alone except to look for him. In the meantime *think* about what I said. Think about what you really want and if you want it with a man who loves you."

Without waiting for her response, he walked through the door to the back of the store and up the stairs to the living quarters, got his coat, hat and gun. Time to put Jordan to rest.

CHAPTER 7

He was tired of living in a hovel. This side of town, Chinatown, was cheap and getting lost along with everyone else trying to hide from whatever or whoever was chasing them was easy. Jordan wouldn't have to do it much longer.

He'd been watching Zach Anderson. The man who had cold-cocked him and started his life down its current path. He's the one that Jordan really needed to kill. He's the one who took away Jordan's life's work.

The life he'd had since the war. That was when he discovered the pleasure he got from killing. In a way, the war had been blessing. He'd always felt out of place before that. But the Army and the War suited him. He was good at it. Yes, it was a sick need, but the taking of lives was the only thing he was good at. The only thing that made him special. If only his father knew how special he'd become.

If Jordan had known Captain Zachariah Anderson was the brother of the man he wanted arrested, he never would have taken him or his unit along to seize the witness. It was the worst piece of luck Jordan had ever had. That started all of this, his bad-luck streak, his running, the end of his career, the end of his *pleasure*.

Now all he could do was kill the Andersons and try to get back his life as another persona. But the Andersons had the best luck of any men he'd ever seen. They hit the biggest vein of gold in the territory; they were finding women to marry and living their happy little lives, while Jordan lived in squalor. It wasn't fair. Time to put some bad luck into their merry little lives.

He dressed with care. Shaved his head and face, so he looked completely different than he did when he was a colonel with his close-cropped hair and mustache, or when he'd nearly gotten caught at the cabin with long hair and full, bushy beard.

ZACH

His black overcoat was so dirty it looked brown and hung two sizes too big. Suspenders kept up the pants that matched the coat. His hat was dusty and ragged, and his boots had holes in the soles. He definitely looked the part of a down on his luck miner. No one would look twice at him, not even the holier-than-thou Anderson brothers.

~*~

The bell over the door rang, and she watched the man meander up to the counter. By now, Lily should be used to the dirty condition of the miners when they came in, but sometimes, she was still surprised and disgusted by them. Couldn't they at least wash their face and hands when they came to town?

She plastered on a smile. "Good day, sir. How can I help you today?"

"Well, ma'am. I've got me a little gold dust here and want to know if I can get the supplies on this list with it."

"Why don't we weigh the dust and then determine just what you can afford."

"Yes, ma'am. Here it is."

The grubby man handed her a small bag.

She took it and weighed it on her scales.

"It's not a lot, about ten dollars worth.

Now let's see that list."

The man handed her the scrap of paper.

Lily couldn't help but notice his clean hands and fingernails. Definitely not the hands of a miner. She cocked her head and glanced quickly at the man, not letting on that she thought anything was amiss.

"Well, you can get the flour, sugar, coffee, and beans. I'll even throw in a tin of peaches, but that will take all the gold you have, I'm afraid you can't afford the bacon. Would you like to do that?" She smiled at the man.

"Yes, ma'am. Mighty kind of you."

"I try to help out when I can," said Lily. "I'm out of business if not for you miners."

He nodded.

Lily wiped her sweating hands on her apron, hoped the man didn't notice, and went about measuring and weighing the goods. She got a tin of peaches and watched him put all the goods into his pack.

"Thankee, ma'am. Mighty good of ya to help out a poor miner."

"You're welcome. Come back again soon."

"You can count on it," he said, his accent gone, as he gathered up his pack and walked out of the store.

Lily leaned against the counter, her legs shaking and her breath coming in pants. That was no miner. Oh, my God. She had to tell Zach. She'd just seen Richard Jordan, and the very fact he felt confident enough to walk into her store frightened her to death.

Zach didn't come home that night or the next. By the third night, when he walked into the house, Lily was beside herself with fright. She flew into his arms, ignoring the dust that covered him and now covered her dressing gown.

He dropped his saddle bags and enveloped her in his embrace. "Lily. What's the matter?"

"Oh, Zach. He was here." She couldn't keep a tremor from her voice.

"Who? Who was here?"

"Him. Richard Jordan. The man you're looking for. He was here. In the store." She was crying now and couldn't seem to stop. After what seemed like forever, he was finally home and all she wanted was to stay secure in his arms.

He held her, resting his cheek on the top of her head, and let her cry.

Finally, she hiccupped and pulled back,

out of his arms.

"I'm sorry," she said, wiping her eyes with the sleeves of her robe. "I've been so frightened. I was sure he knew that I knew who he was and would be back. But he hasn't been and that's almost worse." She swallowed hard. "Not knowing if he would come, or if you would ever be back or not."

"I shouldn't have walked out like I did. I'm sorry, honey. I was angry, and it was best at the time that I left."

She shook her head. "No. I don't blame you. I blame me. I shouldn't have used you to get rid of Beauregard like I did. My act was unfair to you and I'm so sorry."

"You don't have to be sorry. " He smiled and reached for her, "all you have to do is marry me. Is that so hard? I know you love me."

She backed away, farther out of his reach. "How can you be so sure of that? I thought I loved Beauregard and now I know I didn't. How can I be sure that I love you? How can I be sure it's real? I'm afraid, Zach."

He lowered his arms, took off his hat, hung it on a peg and then ran his hand back through his hair before he spoke. "Lily, I'm here. I'm ready to help you. I'll be here for you. What else can you want of me?"

"I don't know." The anguish in her voice surprised her. "I wish I did, but I just don't know."

Watching her pace the length of the floor, he said, "Let's not talk about that right now. Why don't you tell me what you saw with Jordan? How did you recognize him?"

"His hands were clean."

Zach cocked his head. "His hands were clean?"

"Yes. The rest of him was filthy. Just like every other miner that comes in." She gestured at her body as she spoke. "He spoke with an accent and he had ragged clothes and hat. Holes in his boots. And he was bald. No hair on his head or his face. And when he said he'd be back, his accent was gone."

"Lily. I don't think it was Jordan. He's not bald and he's not a miner. I think you were just worried because I was gone, and your imagination got the better of you."

"Don't you *see?*" she insisted, grabbing his arm. "It was him. He *wanted* me to see him. I think he's disguised himself and wanted to see if it worked. He's planning something Zach and I'm afraid."

He lifted his brow and subtly shook his head. She could tell that he still didn't believe her.

"I'd like for him to come back while I'm here," he said. "Right now the best thing for me to do is to continue to try and find him. I'll come home every night, so you won't have to worry, but I need to be out there searching. The sooner I find him the better."

She nodded. It didn't matter what she said, he wouldn't believe she'd seen him. But, her stomach tied in knots, she knew...knew that Jordan was playing with them, specifically with her.

He liked to scare her. She was sure he knew who she was, and that Zach was her boarder. Or more likely he believed, as most people in Deadwood did that Zach was her lover. Jordan wouldn't be trying to frighten her otherwise. He was sending Zach a message—*no one is safe from me.*

~*~

The next morning Zach went to the bath house first thing.

Richardson was up and had the business open at six o'clock.

After the bath he put on clean clothes and took his dirty ones back upstairs and put them in his laundry bag, ready to go to the Chinaman, Wu, for cleaning. Now that he could afford it, he no longer did his own laundry.

He thought more about what Lily said. What if she was right? What if the miner, the disheveled man, was Jordan and he was toying with them?

Why was he so certain Lily was mistaken? Confronting her would be something that Jordan would do if he thought he was safe and since Zach hadn't found him, he probably felt pretty safe.

If Lily was right and the miner was Jordan, then he had to ask himself where he would go to hide. In Deadwood the best place would be Chinatown. You would stand out from the Chinese, but lots of white men were there as well. There were the opium dens, the cheap prostitutes, and flop houses where no one asked any questions. The perfect place for a man on the run to hide.

Taking his laundry there would give Zach the excuse he needed to look around and he wouldn't be gone for too long. He'd been staying close to make Lily feel as safe as possible. As for the laundry, he'd take hers and Gemma's, too. Lily needed the break and the gesture was something little he could do for her—that she might actually let him do.

If she'd let him, he'd hire all the help she needed for both the house and the store. But she was independent. She wouldn't depend on him or anyone else for things she could do herself. At least, not on a regular basis. She might let him get her laundry done once in a while, but that was all.

He picked up his laundry bag. Might as well start now.

"Lily?" he said, entering the kitchen before breakfast. He smelled the coffee boiling and the bacon frying and knew she was up. "I'm taking my laundry to Chinatown. Let me take yours and Gemma's, too. My treat. You could use the extra time to spend with Gemma."

"You always know what to say to make me give in," she said from the stove. She was dressed already for work in a white blouse and black skirt. She wore a small bustle, unusual in Deadwood, as most women found them to be in the way of their work.

He shook his head. "If I really could get

you to give in to me, you'd be my wife already."

"Zach..."

He grinned. "I know, you won't say yes, but don't expect me to stop asking." He loved the look she got when he said the words.

She rolled her eyes and, with a smile and a small shake of her head went back to making breakfast.

~*~

Jordan stood at the window of his little room above the Chinese laundry and shaved his head as he did every morning. This day, he was lucky enough to spy Zach Anderson. He watched Anderson come down the street toward him. If there had been fewer people so he had a clear shot, he might have tried it, even though he wasn't very good with a rifle.

As it was, he watched Anderson approach carrying two bulging laundry bags. Jordan was fairly sure he wasn't coming after him, at least this time. He didn't think this hidey hole had been discovered, and that was a good thing. He wasn't ready with his plans, and running again would necessitate starting over. That he really didn't want to do. Especially not now. Not when everything was falling into place so perfectly.

He walked back away from the window and back to the commode with the mirror above it. He reached into the basin full of water and rinsed the straight razor in his hand. Then he brought it slowly but surely over his scalp, scraping away the stubble until his entire scalp was free of hair.

She'd surely told Anderson of his visit. He made sure she knew it was him, unless she was so dimwitted she couldn't take the hint he'd given. No, the Sutter woman was smart. He'd seen it in her eyes, when she'd realized who he was. She did her best not to let on, but he saw the change, the flicker of recognition in her gaze. Saw the slight tremor in her hand when she handed him the peaches. That was one of the funnier things that had happened; she'd thrown in the can of peaches, hoping he'd leave the store quicker. He smiled, even now as he reached for those same peaches. They'd make a good breakfast.

Poor Anderson, he was so close and yet, so far away.

CHAPTER 8

Zach returned to the mercantile from his trip to Chinatown with new resolve.

"Lily, I'm back." The bell sounded as he entered the store.

She smiled. "Glad you're here. Gemma and I were thinking we could have a picnic, like we used to when Hannah came to play. She's only got a few remaining spots and isn't contagious any more. There's left-over fried chicken and biscuits and I can make some potato salad, and we've got a couple of fresh apples, too. What do you think?"

"Sounds great," he agreed. "After that, I want to take Gemma to Liam and Ellie's to stay for a while."

He saw the moment Lily understood what

he wasn't saying.

"You think he'll come after us…her…don't you?"

She was calm, too calm.

He put his apron over his head and tied it around his waist. "What I'm saying is, I believe you. I believe he was here and was sending me a message. I want Gemma safe. Liam has armed guards protecting his family. If I could, I'd send you, too, but I know you won't go."

"You're right." She gestured toward the room. "This is my business. Next to Gemma, it's the most important thing in my life. I support us with this store. I'm not leaving."

"I knew that's what you'd say, so I hadn't planned on asking, but I still want Gemma to go." *I may take her anyway. She's got to be safe.*

"If you think it's necessary in order to keep her safe, then I want her to go, too. I trust your judgment."

He let out a pent up breath. She'd agreed.

"Go where?" said Gemma upon entering from the back room.

"To Hannah's. Won't that be fun?" asked Lily with a forced smile.

"Yes. When do I get to go?" She jumped up and down with excitement.

"Today after lunch," said Zach, unable to keep from smiling.

Gemma ran in little circles around Zach and Lily. "Yay! I get to go see Hannah."

"Good. Let's have that picnic and get her to Liam's." Zach rolled up his sleeves and prepared to work in the store.

~*~

Today was the box lunch social. Lily prepared her lunch of fried chicken, potato salad, buttermilk biscuits and, because it was Zach's favorite, apple pie for dessert. She packed it all up in a basket, put a slip of paper with her name on top of the pie and tied a bright blue ribbon around the handles, so he'd know which one to bid on.

Having finally bought a new dress, she dressed with extra care. It was light blue serge with dark satin trim around the high collar and long cuffs. The garment was the nicest thing she'd owned since before the War of Northern Aggression. Gathering her gloves, she checked her reflection in the full-length, cheval mirror in the corner of her bedroom.

Her mother's beautiful mirror had been at her brother, Horace's house, a gift for his wife, when the Yankee's burned Lily's home. Horace gave the mirror to Lily when his wife died four years ago. She was still surprised that it had made the trip west, but like her, the mirror was stronger than it looked.

She walked into the kitchen and heard a low whistle.

"You look beautiful."

Lily felt the warmth in her cheeks.

Zach stood next to the stove with the coffee pot in one hand and a cup in the other. The man looked pretty darn handsome himself. He wore a crisp, white shirt with black wool trousers and vest. His black cravat was tied perfectly. His hair slicked straight back made his blue eyes stand out in sharp contrast to his dark hair.

"You look pretty good yourself. No woman at church today will be able to concentrate on the good reverend's sermon. They'll all be vying for your attention so you'll buy their lunch."

He walked over and took her by the waist. "Flattery will get you everywhere."

He brought her close.

She leaned back her head and lifted her face, in anticipation of his kiss. Lucky for her, she didn't have to wait long. His lips touched hers, soft and gentle. When she responded and kissed him back, he pulled her closer, kissing her thoroughly, completely. She was breathless when he finally raised his head.

"Oh, my." They were the only words she could think of. Her brain was mush.

He chuckled. "Glad to see I still have that effect on you."

"You always have an effect on me, and you know it."

He smiled. "Good to know. Now, is that your basket?"

She picked the basket off the counter. "This is it. Full of your favorites."

"Yum. I can't wait. One basket with a blue ribbon. I can remember that."

They got to the reverend's tent in time to set down their basket with the others and take a seat before he began his sermon.

Lily looked at the other boxed lunch offerings and saw no less than three other baskets, exactly like hers, and tied with various shades of blue ribbon. She shouldn't have been surprised. Everyone got their baskets and ribbon at the mercantile. Duplicates were bound to occur. She should have tied it with a piece of an old dress so the color wouldn't be duplicated. Now someone other than Zach could get her basket and he might be having lunch with someone else, too.

The sermon seemed to last forever and she only half-listened. When it was finally over, Ellie Anderson rose and walked to the front of the tent.

"I'm so pleased to see everyone here today. We have folks we don't normally get to see, and I say welcome to you. Now shall we get started with the auction?"

A resounding "yes" sounded from the crowd.

Ellie grabbed the first offering—a large basket, just like Lily's, tied with a bright red ribbon.

"What am I bid for this lovely basket?"

A flurry of bidding took place between two men. One was a miner from the looks of him, and the other was the butcher.

Lily was surprised because she thought the butcher was a married man, though if she thought about past instances, she'd never seen his wife.

The butcher won with a forty dollar bid. The owner of the basket was a lovely brown-haired woman. Lily thought she was a widow, though she didn't know what she did for a living. Maybe the woman took in laundry or sewing. She'd have to find out because she could use a good seamstress. Gemma was growing faster than Lily could get the clothes into the store.

The first of the four baskets like Lily's came up for bid.

"Is that yours?" asked Zach.

"I don't know for sure, but I don't think so. The color of the ribbon's not right."

"Okay. I won't bid on it."

They watched the bidding on more lunches. The winners and owners of the baskets either sat in the tent or left for more private places to be together.

The next blue-ribboned basket came up.

"Oh," said Lily, stretching out of her seat to see better. "I think that's mine but I can't be sure."

"Do you want me to bid on it? What if it's not yours?"

"Well, if it's not mine, you'll be having lunch with someone else."

His brows wrinkled. "I don't like that idea or the fact that you'll be with someone other than me. Even if it is for a good cause and just for lunch."

"Wait on this one. I...I don't think it's mine, after all."

They waited and Zach didn't bid. The basket turned out not to be Lily's and they both breathed a sigh of relief.

When the third basket with a blue ribbon came up, Lily said, "This is it. I'm pretty sure that's my basket. I want you to bid on it."

"Okay. Twenty dollars," shouted Zach.

"Thirty," said a voice with a thick Southern drawl.

Zach and Lily both looked over their shoulders to see Beauregard Parkerson sitting two rows behind them.

"Fifty," said Zach.

"One hundred," said Parkerson.

"Wonderful. Do I have one twenty?" said Ellie.

"Two hundred," said Zach.

Parkerson shook his head.

"Sold for two hundred to Mr. Zach Anderson," said Ellie, pulling the slip of paper from the basket. "Whose lunch do we have here? Miss Scarlet Rogers."

Zach rose, "Stay where I can see you." He went to meet Miss Rogers. She was an employee of *The Gem*. A beautiful raven-haired woman, she was dressed in a low-cut burgundy velvet dress with black lace trim.

Lily clamped her jaw shut and pursed her lips. How could this happen?

The next basket was Lily's. It had to be. It was the last one with a blue ribbon.

"Twenty dollars," said Parkerson.

"Thirty dollars," said a grubby miner.

"Fifty," replied Parkerson.

"Too rich for my blood," said the red haired miner with a shake of his head.

"Sold for fifty dollars. And who do we have?" Ellie read from the slip of paper, "Lily Sutter."

Parkerson grinned.

Lily frowned. *How could this happen? Did Beauregard do something to the ribbons?*

He came over to her carrying the basket he'd won.

"What are you still doing here, Beauregard? You should have left when Zach told you to."

"I've told you to call me Beau," he said through gritted teeth. He closed his eyes and pinched the bridge of his nose and said more cordially, "It's a free country, my dear Lily, and I came here to pan for gold. I plan on staying. Finding you here was a bonus and I've learned there's a child I need to get acquainted with.

"Do you see a child?" she waved a hand around her. "I was lying to you when I said I was pregnant. I just wanted to get married to you. For some reason I fancied myself in love with you. I don't any more. I don't want to marry you, I don't want you anywhere near me. You make my skin crawl."

"Really? We'll see." He narrowed his gaze and reached for her arm to help her up from her chair. "In the meantime, I think you and I should get reacquainted."

Lily pulled her arm from his grasp. "That's not happening. I told you I'm engaged to Zach."

She watched Beauregard's gaze rise to something behind her and widen.

"That's right. She's engaged to me. Now, I've arranged for you to have lunch with the delightful Miss Rogers, who is more your type…mercenary. So go quietly to the lady, or have me beat you to a pulp in front of all these nice, church going people."

"You wouldn't dare," said Parkerson,

raising his chin just a bit.

"Try me," said Zach as he unbuttoned his coat.

"All right. I'm going, but don't think this is over. I'm still coming back for my child," he hissed. "You can't keep it from me. It's mine."

Zach and Lily watched him walk away toward Miss Rogers.

"What will we do? What happens when he truly finds out about Gemma?" whispered Lily when they turned back to the lunch, still in the basket.

"Marry me, Lily. Let me be Gemma's daddy for real. Let me have the legal right to protect both of you."

"I...I—" *I miss Gemma, our story time together. If I married Zach, maybe I could bring her home.*

He took her hand, "—Just think about it. In the meantime I'll pay a visit to our rebel friend."

Lily was shaking from head to toe, feeling like she'd just been doused with cold water. She nodded. Words eluded her. Beauregard scared her. If he knew Gemma was his, what lengths would he go to in order to use that against Lily?

~*~

Interesting things were happening with the Sutter woman. She had another suitor — apparently an unwanted suitor if the scene he just observed at the box lunch social was any indication.

Jordan knew Anderson and the dear Lily would attend the social. How could they not when the event was being orchestrated by his sister-in-law for her father's church?

In a bit of dangerous activity, Jordan had actually bid on Lily's basket, once he'd known it was hers and that Anderson had won the wrong basket. But Lily's new suitor had seemed determined and Jordan didn't want to call attention to himself. Around the corner of the nearest building, in the alley, he removed the red wig and beard he'd pilfered from the theater troupe. It had proved to be an effective disguise. He'd have to use it more often to keep an eye on this new man. The stranger could get in the way and muck things up.

Jordan couldn't…wouldn't let that happen.

And where was the child? Had Jordan's visit scared Lily so much she'd sent away the little girl? Or was she hiding…Gemma…that was her name, from someone else? Perhaps this Parkerson fellow.

Jordan knew Lily had a child out of wedlock, the knowledge wasn't secret. All of the town knew. Was this new man the father? He was from the south like Lily and, given his familiarity with her, the possibility seemed likely.

He would have to keep a close watch on this man.

No one would interfere with his plans for Zach Anderson. No one.

~*~

After the social, Zach and Lily went with Liam and Ellie back to their house. The kids were there with men Liam hired to guard them. They all thought bringing any of the children to the social was dangerous and, Lily was adamant Parkerson know nothing about Gemma. Beauregard could calculate that based on her age and her similarity to Lily, Gemma was his child. Unless...*could she do it? Could she say that Zach was Gemma's father?*

Zach would attest to it, and Gemma already loved him like a father. Was Lily being selfish by not accepting Zach's proposals of marriage? Was she letting her former liaison with Beauregard cloud the relationship she could have with Zach? Of course, she was. But how to stop? Learning to trust was not easy. How could she trust Zach to keep her heart safe?

That night, she tossed and turned in her sleep. She dreamed about marrying Zach. Then the dream turned to a nightmare when Zach had turned into Beauregard. She was so frightened, she'd awakened in a cold sweat.

Unable to go back to sleep, she got up and went to the kitchen. She lit the stove and was putting on the tea kettle when Zach came in.

"I thought I heard you up. Couldn't sleep?"

She nodded. "I had a nightmare. Want some tea? I hope it'll help me go back to sleep."

"Sure. Want to talk about it?"

Shaking her head, she said, "No. That will just make it seem real."

"Alright. We won't talk about it. Let's talk about us and about what we'll do to keep Gemma, *and you*, safe. Not just from Parkerson, but from Jordan as well."

"I've given it a lot of thought and—"

"—and," said Zach, leaning close.

She knew she shouldn't keep him waiting but the decision had not been an easy one.

Turning her back to him, she said, "I've decided to take you up on your offer of marriage. You're right. Getting married is the only way I can keep Gemma safe and she already loves you like a father."

Zach came up behind her, wrapped his arms around her waist and pulled her back against him. "And what about you? Do you love me?"

She wanted to answer a resounding *yes*, but she couldn't. Giving someone, even Zach, that kind of power over her was too frightening. Admitting her feelings to him made her vulnerable, and she couldn't do that.

"Love isn't in my vocabulary. Not for anyone but Gemma."

He stiffened behind her, but then relaxed and kissed her neck.

"I intend to change your mind about that. You're safe with me Lily, and so is your heart. I won't hurt you."

She pulled away and wrapped her arms around herself. "You say that and I'm sure you mean it, but it won't work that way. You'll hurt me Zach, I know that."

He slightly shook his head and narrowed his eyes. "Then why?"

"I told you. For Gemma."

He shook his head. "That's a nice excuse, but there are other ways to protect Gemma and you know it. I could just have Parkerson disappear. Plenty of men in Deadwood would be willing to do it for a bottle of whiskey much less the gold to buy it."

She gasped. "You would never do that. You're not that kind of man."

"If I'm the kind of man who would hurt you, like you believe, then why wouldn't I be the kind who would make Parkerson disappear?"

He was close to shouting and his words were harsh. Maybe she deserved them. She was scared, but perhaps it was time to face that fear.

"I let my heart have free reign once and it was thrown aside. The only thing good to come from that experience was Gemma. Forgive me if I'm reluctant to take the slightest chance it could happen again." She straightened she shoulders and stiffened her back. "I promised myself that I wouldn't let a man have that much influence over me, over my life and I don't intend to. Even now that I've agreed to marry you, it doesn't mean I'll let myself be dominated by you or that I'll risk my heart. I won't be hurt like that again by anyone."

Zach listened to Lily's determined words. He heard the fear behind them and knew he couldn't push her. Not now. He was sure she loved him, but also sure she didn't realize it, too scared and unsure of herself and her feelings to give in to them again. He understood, but that didn't stop him from hurting a little at her words.

Instead, he led her over to the divan and they sat. He kept his arm around her and gently tugged her over until she rested her head against his shoulder.

"We need to talk to Reverend Smith right away. The sooner, the better. We'll grab Jake and Becky, get married, and then go see Liam, so he and Ellie know what's going on and why. We all have to keep our stories straight. We all have to agree on Gemma being my daughter, and that I've just found you again."

"Beauregard will be wary of a story about a Yankee officer sweeping me off my feet, knowing how I felt about Yankees."

"No one knows that we met only ten months ago, or that I was thunderstruck by you."

She blushed at his words and he smiled.

"We'll say we met six years ago. I wasn't in uniform." He took a minute, chewing on the inside of his lip like he did when he was deep in thought. "You met me by the creek, while I was fishing; when you came down to fish yourself. Didn't you do that? Fish, I mean."

"Well, yes, I did. Food was still hard to come by, even though the war was long over. At least to the damn Yankees it was over," she added under her breath.

"Tsk. Tsk. That's an attitude you have to get over."

"What?"

"Referring to me as a damn Yankee." He smiled when he said it, but it was none the less true.

"You know I haven't done that." She smiled back at him then dropped her gaze. "Well, maybe when I'm alone."

"Alright then. Did you ever go fishing with Parkerson?"

"Beauregard? Go fishing?" As she shook her head, she laughed. "He couldn't stand the thought of getting his hands dirty. He must be desperate to be here in Deadwood. It does explain why he suddenly wants me so much, since he didn't before. At least after the one time. He smells money."

He watched her blush.

Zach picked up on the hurt and disgust but one line stood out to him.

"One time. You only made love one time before getting pregnant with Gemma? You are a fertile flower."

"If that was making love then I'm not interested in ever doing it again. Coupling was horrible."

Zach pulled back and took her sweet face between his palms, very gently, allowing her to pull away at any time. "Oh, my darling, you have no idea about actually making love. You had sex and not very good sex by the sound of it. There is so much pleasure to be had in joining with someone you care about. Making love is so much more than just sex."

As he watched, he could see her resolve waver, replaced by curiosity.

"You like it when I do this, don't you?" He lowered his lips to hers and softly kissed her. Not pushing for entry, but slowly savoring her. When he pulled back he heard her sigh.

Raising her gaze to his, she nodded

vigorously. "Yes, I do."

"Just think of that pleasure."

Her eyes closed, a smile played at the edge of her lips.

"Multiplied a thousand times."

Her eyes popped open, then widened.

He saw definite interest on her beautiful face.

"You're teasing me. That's not possible."

"It's true. I swear to you. I will give you so much pleasure, you'll never think of that first time again."

She cocked an eyebrow. "You're awfully sure of yourself."

He grinned. He couldn't help it. "After we're married, with your permission, I'll please you in ways you can only imagine. I will make love to you and, if we're lucky, we'll start another child as beautiful as you and Gemma."

She ducked her head. "I wouldn't be opposed to a child who took after you."

Zach saw her lips turn up. Shaking his head sadly, he said, "Highly unlikely. Usually it happens only once in a generation, and we have our Hannah already."

"But it could happen," she persisted, her

gaze searching his face.

He cocked an eyebrow, "So...you want more children?"

"Of course, I do. I'm even willing to endure coupling in order to get them."

He chuckled. "Trust me, love, you won't be enduring, you'll be enjoying."

"We'll see."

He was quite pleased with himself. He'd taken her from hating the prospect of lovemaking to admitting she wanted more children. That was progress, and he knew after their first time together she'd want more. He'd see to it.

Maybe, if he was lucky, she'd realize she was in love with him, like he was with her. He didn't know when it happened. Maybe the first time he'd seen her. After that, love just sort of wafted over him like a slow-moving fog. Covering him completely, blocking his vision to anyone but her.

CHAPTER 9

Zach and Lily arrived on Jake's front porch three hours after the Sunday service ended, both of them still wearing their Sunday best.

Jake answered the door, smiling wide when he saw them. "Come in. Come in. What brings you two by this afternoon?"

"Lily and I are getting married, and want you and Becky to stand up for us," stated Zach before Lily could speak.

Jake stood there stunned for a moment, then he looked at Lily. "I thought you told Becky you'd never marry this jackass as long as you live." He nodded toward his brother.

Zach turned to Lily and cocked his eyebrow in question. "Jackass?"

She blushed, but raised her chin in

defiance. "I didn't know you. It was how I felt about every man then, especially the handsome ones."

His mouth turned up at the corners. "Flattery will get you everywhere."

She swatted his arm.

He was glad to see her tease him when their world was about to take a very serious turn. Marriage, at least to him, was forever. He'd never done it in all his thirty-eight years, for a reason. Until Lily, he'd never wanted to take the chance, never wanted to risk everything, risk his heart, on one other person. But he had faith in Lily. He loved her and eventually she would realize she loved him, too. It was just a matter of time. He was sure of her feelings. He had to be.

When Jake, Becky and baby Jenny were ready to go, they all went to Reverend Smith's tent hoping the good reverend was inside.

Zach poked his head through the flap. "Reverend Smith? Are you here?"

"I am, son. Come in."

He held back the tent flap and let everyone pass in front of him before letting it close behind him.

"Reverend," said Zach, as he approached

the somber-looking man in the worn black suit. "Lily and I would like to get married. Today. Now. We brought our witnesses."

"What is it with you Anderson boys?" The tall, thin man, with graying brown hair, rose from the table he used as a desk and a pulpit. "You are always in such a hurry to wed."

Zach grinned and put his arm around Lily. "We want to make sure the right girl doesn't get away."

The reverend shook his head, picked up his bible and motioned for them to come forward.

Zach and Lily stood in front of him, Lily on Zach's left, Becky next to her, holding Jenny. Jake was on Zach's right.

"Do you have a ring?" asked Jake.

Zach nodded. "I bought it when I started courting Lily. I knew someday she'd be my bride." Out of his pocket he pulled a thick band of gold and diamonds.

Lily stared at Zach. "How could you know? I didn't even know until today."

"I told you. I had faith. What about you? Do you have a ring?"

She nodded. "It was my daddy's." From her pocket, she pulled a well worn, slim, plain gold band.

"It's perfect," said Zach and couldn't resist bending to kiss her.

"Mr. Anderson," said the reverend. "There will be plenty of time for that *after* the ceremony."

"Ah, yes sir. Sorry." Zach was sure he was red. He felt like a boy who had just been scolded for getting caught with his hand in the cookie jar.

"Now," said Reverend Smith. "We are gathered here, in front of these witnesses, to join this man and this woman…"

The serious tone filtered through Lily's thoughts. She was marrying Zach. The reverend said the words, she heard them and responded.

"I do," she said at the proper time.

Zach must have said the right things, too, because before she knew it, the reverend said, "I now pronounce you man and wife."

She looked up at Zach. He was smiling, and then he leaned down and kissed her. This kiss was different than his others. It was soft, and yet filled with promise of things to come.

~*~

Jordan packed his belongings into a single

worn valise. These possessions were all that was left, all he could get his hands on when he'd had to run from Ft. Leavenworth, Kansas. He'd only escaped just before Liam Anderson had shown up…with six soldiers in tow. Then he'd run, but not far, just enough to stay out of Anderson's way, but close enough to follow him when he left to return home. Here. To Deadwood.

Jordan wasn't running now. He was leading. Leading his prey to him. He'd have to appear at the general store again, get Zach's attention and lead him to the alley where he had a surprise waiting.

Yes, it was time to start eliminating them. He'd leave Jake for last. After all, he was the one who had denied Jordan completion. Denied him seeing the light, the life, leave the woman's eyes. Jake Anderson was who owed him the most and he would pay.

First though, would be Zach, because he was still searching for Jordan. Now he'd let himself be found, well, just long enough so Jordan could ambush him. He needed Zach out of the way. Then he could take the child. The rest of the brothers would come running at the loss of a child. Especially one of *their* children.

He'd tried taking the woman, Ellie, but that hadn't worked. All that act had done was make him run, with Zach on his tail, until he could return, unseen. He knew that they knew he was there, but they didn't know where he was. And with the changes he'd made to his appearance, he'd been able to walk right under their noses without them detecting him.

But they'd taken away the little girl because of that Parkerson fellow. He might have to get rid of the southern interloper, but then again, that would only draw attention to Jordan. Who else would kill Parkerson? Maybe Zach. The Anderson brother didn't seem to like him much, from what Jordan had observed at the Sunday social. Maybe he'd kill him. That would make getting to the child easier. He'd have to watch and see. When his opportunity arose, he'd take it. Whether to kill Zach Anderson, or to snatch his little girl. One would come up and he'd take advantage of whichever it might be.

They won't stop me this time.

~*~

Zach and Lily went with Jake and Becky back to their house.

"Now that the deed is done, can you tell

me why you two were in such an all-fired hurry to get married?" asked Jake.

"We want to protect Gemma," said Zach. He curled his hat brim with his fingers, realized what he was doing and stopped. "We'll say she's *my* daughter. She looks exactly like Lily, so there is nothing there to say she's not mine. We don't want Parkerson to have any claim on her."

"Woohoo," whistled Jake. "That's still taking an awful chance. Folks will wonder why you didn't marry before now."

"Everyone knows I've been trying to get Lily to marry me since day one. Now they'll have a reason why. They'll think I followed Lily here, and it's taken all this time to convince her to marry me. Which it has."

"And why wouldn't she have married you before, if you're Gemma's father," asked Becky. She held Jenny, walking and patting her back. The baby was fussy and Becky was trying to ease her.

"Here, let me have her," said Lily holding up her hands for Jenny.

Becky obliged.

Lily sat and laid the baby tummy first across her knees. Then she moved her knees back and forth and rubbed the baby's back. In a short time, Jenny gave a large burp and settled contentedly across Lily's lap. Lily put a diaper over her shoulder to protect her dress and placed the baby against the diaper. She stood and began to walk, swaying to the tune of a song she hummed.

"I'd forgotten how small and needy they are at this age. Or that special, sweet scent, fresh from a bath. You can still smell it in her hair," Lily said, as she sniffed Jenny's baby soft hair.

"I like to bathe her every day. I spent too many years of only having spit baths. A real bath was a luxury, I couldn't often afford." Becky stood next to Lily and gently rubbed Jenny's head. "My daughter is never going to know that kind of hardship, if I can help it."

Jake put his arm around his wife's shoulder and brought her close. "Never. We can bathe whenever we want, sometimes all three of us together."

Zach pinched the bridge of his nose. "That is not what I want to hear. Now I'll never look at your bathtub the same way."

Lily laughed.

The joy in the sound eased Zach's nerves

and he cocked his head toward her.

She had taken the baby to the rocker, cradling her in her arms and rocking her to sleep.

It didn't take long. Jenny's eyes closed almost as soon as Lily started the rocker moving. Jenny recognized a mother when she was held by one.

The sight of her with the baby touched his heart, and he couldn't wait to see her with their baby. A boy with curly blond hair, just like his mother's or a girl, maybe a brown-haired one like Liam. Lily wanted a black-haired baby like he was, but that had never happened as far as he knew. Only one in a generation, but if he could give it to her, he would. He'd give Lily the world, if she'd let him.

"Now back to our story," said Jake. "It has to be right, and we have to all agree on the same thing. Why wouldn't Lily marry you before?"

"Well," began Zach, rubbing a hand over the back of his neck.

"He wasn't true to me," said Lily. "He wasn't ready to settle down and wanted to see other women. They threw themselves at him, and he caught them. It's taken him this long to convince me he's a changed man."

"Should be enough to say she married me," grumbled Zach, not at all happy with Lily's scenario of what could have transpired.

"No, it's not. People want a story. They want the dirt, the juicy bits," countered Lily. "They've butted their nose into my business since I got here. Wanting to know where Gemma's father was. I tried to pass myself off as widowed when I first came to Deadwood, but a man from my hometown showed up and told everyone that was a lie. From then on, I made sure everyone knew I wasn't married and that none of that was Gemma's fault." Still rocking Jenny, she lowered her voice. "Believe it or not, most people here in Deadwood couldn't care less. Once the initial titilation was over, they moved on. It was no longer of interest. Now that Beauregard is here, that could change. I can't afford that. Not for Gemma, and not for my business."

She got up from the rocker and handed Jenny back to Becky.

"Here you go. The sweet thing is just worn out. Give her a sugar teet when she wakes up in between feedings if you want. It'll keep her satisfied and keep air out of her tummy."

"I don't know how to make a sugar teet," admitted Becky.

"It's easy. You just need a dishtowel and a handful of sugar. I'll show you."

"Ladies, pay attention, please," said Jake, drawing them back into the conversation.

"Okay, I'll agree to your story, though I don't like it. There is no way I would ever have treated you like that, but there always has to be a villain. I guess I'm it in this play," said Zach begrudgingly to Lily. *He didn't like it not one bit. It reminded him too much of how he really used to be. Before Lily. He was a whole other person, before Lily.*

They loaded up the wagon with a picnic basket and some supplies they were taking to Liam and Ellie. Zach saddled the big sorrel horse he kept at Jake's and had Lily ride in front of him. He liked the feel of her against him and she didn't seem to mind.

"Are you having second thoughts?" he asked, afraid of the answer.

"No. Are you?" she asked quietly.

"Hell no! I've wanted to marry you since the day I first laid eyes on you. And before you protest, I'm not joking. From day one. Liam had never seen me thunderstruck, like I was with you. I admit the women have always chased me, and I usually answered their offers in the affirmative." He felt her stiffen and pull away but tightened his arm around her belly and brought her right back against his chest. "Until you, Lily. I swear, I haven't even looked at another woman since meeting you."

A moment passed then he felt her relax against him.

"I mean to prove it to you. Whatever you need me to do, I'll do it."

"I don't know, Zach. The arrangement is all still really new and I'm just now getting everything straight in my mind. I don't know what I need from you except for you to just be...*you*...and give me time to adjust."

He didn't much like what she said but he understood it. She'd been alone with Gemma for a long time. Depending on no one but herself for survival. She needed time to trust him and he'd continue to give her that time.

"I loved seeing you with Jenny today. You were meant to have babies, Lily. I hope you'll have lots of babies with me."

Her head bowed.

He knew she blushed.

"I don't know about that. I'm afraid, even

though you've told me I don't need to be. I'm struggling to believe the act can be *pleasurable.*"

He wanted to insist on his husbandly rights, but knew Lily didn't need that. She needed to understand and know that relations between a man and a woman needn't be painful.

"I understand and I want to give you that time, but with a condition."

"What's that?" Her body stiffened.

"We start sleeping in the same bed. I want you to get used to me, to seeing me and being with me. I don't want to remain in the spare room. I need to hold you in my arms and feel your body next to mine."

She shook her head. "I don't know if that is such a good idea. I think it would be best for things to remain as they are." She kept her voice low and her eyes straight ahead.

He tried to keep calm and rested a hand over hers. "Lily, honey, I want to give you the time you need, but I also want you to understand this is going to happen. I want more children and I know you do, too. There's only one way for that to occur, and you need to get used to that fact. I swear to you, I won't hurt you."

She kept her body relaxed against his.

That was progress and he smiled.

"Thank you for marrying me to protect Gemma."

Her words were spoken so quietly he barely heard it over the clip-clop of the horses' hooves against the road.

There were so many things he wanted to say. He wanted to tell her he'd have married her for any reason. The only one that counted was that he loved her and Gemma. He wanted to tell her how much he loved her, but she'd never believe him and just brush aside the words. He wouldn't say the words again until he heard them from her first.

For now he settled for what he knew she needed to hear.

"I love Gemma and would do anything to protect her from harm. The same goes for you, Lily. I will do the best I can to protect you. Always."

They had reached the edge of town and were taking the turn onto the creek road when he felt it. The force shoved him against Lily. The burning in his side was terrible, and he slumped against her back.

"Zach! Zach, what's wrong?!"

He tried to tighten his right arm around her waist but couldn't, the strength was gone. "Lily. I've been shot. Take the reins and call to Jake."

She grabbed the reins from his hands. "Jake! Jake! Hold on. He can't hear me." She kicked the horse's sides until it was moving at a fast walk, and she guided it abreast the wagon's bench seat where Jake and Becky sat.

Jake finally looked over.

"He's been shot. Zach's been shot!" She shouted in order to be heard over the din of horse's hooves striking the hard-packed dirt road, the creaking of wagons and of people talking.

This time, he understood. He pulled the buckboard to a stop, set the brake, jumped down, and came to Lily's side.

"Lean down to me, brother," said Jake as he reached up to help Zach out of the saddle.

His right side was covered in so much blood. Her heart pounded in her chest, Lily couldn't tell where he'd actually been shot.

Jake put himself under Zach's left arm and got him to the wagon where he and Lily helped Zach onto the back of the buckboard. Lily scrambled in and placed Zach's head on her lap, cushioning it and providing what comfort she could. Jake tied the sorrel to the back, turned the wagon toward town and headed to Doc Cochran's place.

When they arrived, Jake drew the buckboard to a halt, set the brake and jumped down. He ran to the doctor's office, pounded on the door and called, "Doc! Doc Cochran!"

Doc's weary face appeared at the window in the door a moment before it swung wide.

"Jake Anderson, what are you doing here? Is Becky alright? The baby?"

"My brother's been shot." Jake ran back to the wagon.

Zach had managed to get down from the wagon bed and was leaning against the side for support.

He was pale and Lily worried he'd fall down, but he refused to let her help him.

"You'll get your dress all bloody."

Exasperated, she said, "Don't be ridiculous. It's already bloody. Who cares?"

Jake came up, ignored Lily and again put himself under Zach's left arm. He helped him into the doctor's office and onto the table in the middle of the main room. The doctor got a basin and forceps before using scissors to cut away Zach's shirt.

"I'd have taken it off, if you'd asked," snapped Zach.

"Nope. I don't think so," replied Doc. "You've been babying your right side because of the pain. I've been watching. On first glance, I'd say you're lucky. The bullet hit you in the side below your shoulder and doesn't appear to have hit your lung. But with this much blood, it may have nicked an artery. I won't know for sure until I get in there and feel around. You want ether?"

"No. I don't like the stuff. Just do it and don't let her watch." Zach nodded toward Lily, who'd come in behind them and quietly waited in the small room that served as waiting room and entrance.

"He's right, Miss Sutter—" began Doc.

"—Mrs. Anderson, Doctor." Lily stepped close. "Zach is my husband and I'll stay."

The door opened and Becky came in with Jenny, the baby wrapped tightly in her arms.

"I'm not staying out there by myself."

"You should go home, both of you," said Lily to Jake, her hands folded demurely in front of her to stop them from shaking.

Jake shook his head. "He's my brother."

"And he's my husband. I'll stay. Take your family home, Jake. I'll send word as soon as I know anything."

"I need Jake to stay," interrupted Doc. "He'll have to hold down Zach if I have to dig out the bullet."

"Jake stays and so do I. Won't be the first time I've seen a bullet taken out of an Anderson," said Becky.

Lily remembered Jake was shot last year, and he'd recovered completely without the doctor to take it out or to treat him. Liam had removed the bullet then. Becky told her all about it. Now, the story gave her hope that Zach would fully recover.

"Very well," sighed the doctor. "You ladies stay where you are, and don't say I didn't warn you."

"Just proceed, Doc. Becky and I will be fine," said Lily.

The doctor stuck his finger into the wound and wiggled it around.

Zach groaned and bit down on the rawhide knife sheath that Jake slid into his mouth. He didn't shout, not even a muted yell, just groaned.

Lily knew he was brave but didn't know if

he was being especially stoic for her benefit or whether he would have been that way anyway. She knew doc's probing must hurt like the dickens, and almost wished he would holler and let all the pain out rather than keep it inside. But she knew he couldn't let the pain overcome him. She may not know a lot of things about her new husband, but she was certain of that. He must remain in control.

"I don't feel a bullet. Looks like it missed the artery, bounced off your rib and exited. That's why there was so much blood. You have two wounds, one entrance and one exit." Doc looked up at Lily and then to Jake. "Our boy here is one lucky son of a bitch. He'll be fine. You'll have to watch him for fever and infection, Lily. But this here will go a long way to prevent that."

He took a bottle of whiskey and poured a goodly amount into the wounds.

"Argg! Dammit, Doc! What are you doing? Torturing me?" shouted Zach. It was the first time he showed pain and she was sure that was because it was unexpected.

"Save you. The alcohol will clean the wounds. Now I'll stitch you up and it'll hurt but nothing like the stuff you've already endured." He looked up at Lily. "Mrs. Anderson, you need to keep the wounds clean and dry. I want the bandages changed every other day and I want to see him again in a week or so."

"Yes, doctor." Lily smiled. She felt lighter than she had most of the day. Now the question of whether the marriage was right, the worry about Beauregard, all that seemed not as important as the fact that Zach would be alright.

She looked at Zach. "We're going home, and you're going to bed. Jake and Becky can fill Liam in on everything."

"Before you all leave, I have one question to ask," said Doc Cochran. He scanned those around the table.

"Yes, sir. What would you like to know?" asked Jake.

"Who shot Zach? Who is so afraid of him that he would shoot him in the back, rather than face him?"

"That's the million dollar question, Doc?" said Zach through gritted teeth.

CHAPTER 10

Zach put his arm around Lily's shoulder and she wrapped her arm around his waist. He didn't want to lean on her, but he was weak from loss of blood. Being shot took more out of him than he wanted to admit. If anyone thought anything about him walking down the street with no shirt on and only a bandage, they didn't mention it. Folks tended to keep to themselves in Deadwood. That would make finding who did this that much harder, but he had a good idea where to start looking.

They reached the store and went up the back stairs. Lily guided him to her bedroom.

"You feeling sorry for me so you're putting me in here?"

"No, I'm not feeling sorry for you. Being in

here is more practical, so I can watch you. And" she took a deep breath, "I remember what you said about sleeping together. I agreed to that when I married you. I'm not backing out now just because you're wounded. Especially not because you're wounded. That would be petty."

He smiled and squeezed her shoulder. "You're one hell of a woman, Lily Anderson."

"Yes, I am and don't you forget it. Now let's get off the rest of your clothes and you into bed."

His right side was pretty useless as the doctor didn't want him straining that side at all and perhaps popping the stitches. So, she helped him with his boots and socks. Then she undid his belt and pulled down his pants, being careful not to grab his underdrawers with them.

"Aren't you afraid I might try to make love to you?" He asked while she pulled down the covers and fluffed the pillows.

"No. You said you wouldn't and I believe you will give me time to get used to you. Besides you're weak as a kitten now and hardly a threat. I'll get the pillows from the other bedroom and prop you up so you'll be comfortable. Then I'll make you some white willow bark tea."

He nodded, disgusted with himself that she was right. He was weak as a kitten. The shot, the loss of blood, all of it took the life right out of him. He leaned back against the pillows, suddenly tired, worn out.

Someone shot him. They could have hit Lily, and that made him madder than the fact they had hit him. *Were they aiming for him or for her? Why would anyone want to kill Lily?* They didn't. They wanted him and he thought he knew who. At least he had two good suspects — Jordan and Parkerson. And he'd put his money on Parkerson. Jordan didn't want to shoot him in the back. He wanted to watch him die. But Parkerson, the act was just like him, coward that he was, to shoot him in the back. He was trying to kill him. He's lucky he didn't hit Lily. Zach would make him pay for this. Make him pay dearly.

Lily came back carrying two pillows.

"Here now, let me put these behind you."

He sat upright but couldn't help a groan of pain.

"I intend to talk to Mrs. Ferguson about watching the store while I tend to you. She's done it before when Gemma's been sick."

"I don't need tending. I'm perfectly capable of taking care of myself." He wouldn't admit he needed help, even if he did.

"Of course, you are," she said on her way out the door.

Minutes later, she returned with a cup and saucer.

"Here is the willow bark tea. I added honey to make it tolerable. It's bitter otherwise."

She handed him the cup and set the saucer on the night table next to the bed.

"It's still bitter," he grumbled.

"Drink it anyway," she said, raising her eyebrows and nodding at the cup.

"I think Parkerson is the one who shot me." He kept his gaze on her. If there was any surprise there, he didn't see it.

"I thought as much myself. It would be something he would do. He knows he can't get around you to get to me, so he figured he'd just take you out of the picture all together."

"I will make him pay for this. He could have hit you!"

She sat on the side of the bed next to him. "Considering he's probably not a very good shot, I'm surprised he didn't. He's desperate, Zach. That makes him dangerous."

"Yeah. Just like a wounded animal, and like that animal, he needs to be put down."

"Try not to kill him. Doing so wouldn't be good for you." She patted his leg like he was a small child.

"Not be good for me? It'll be very good for me." He barely kept down his voice. If he wasn't feeling so bad, he'd be yelling.

"You're not a murderer, Zach," said Lily in a calm tone. "Don't let him turn you into one."

He took a deep breath. "What do you propose that I do? Just let him go?"

"Well, no," she said, uncertainty in her voice. "But can't you give him over to the sheriff?"

"We don't have any proof that he did this, unless I beat it out of him."

She placed her hand on his chest.

At her touch, he immediately felt calmer. How could she have that effect on him? Had to be because he loved her so much. Just her touch resonated through him, comforting him, healing him.

"You're not that kind of man."

She said it softly but he could tell she

believed it. She believed the best of him.

"You're wrong. I'm just that kind of man. Ask Jake. I brought him to Liam's at gunpoint."

"That's different, he's your brother and he knew you wouldn't really shoot. Beauregard is afraid of you. He doesn't know you."

"Lily, you don't know me either if you think I'm letting Parkerson get away with this. He could have killed you." Zach swallowed hard before he could continue. "He's damn lucky he didn't kill me, though I'm sure he doesn't think so. Liam and Jake wouldn't be so easy on him if he'd killed me. I won't kill him, but I'll sure as hell make him wish I had."

She rose from the bed, her back stiff as a board. "You'll do what you have to. I know that, yet I am not resigned that you will kill him."

He saw the torment in her eyes and sought to alleviate it. "I told you I won't kill him. Honest." He crossed his heart like a child would. "Does that make you feel better?"

"Yes," she said, her stance relaxing. "As much as I hate the man, I don't want you to lower yourself to his standards. Let the law handle the problem."

He wouldn't tell her he intended to beat the living daylights out of dear Beauregard before sending him back to Georgia. They had no proof he was the one who shot Zach, but that didn't mean he'd let him get away with it. Proof or not.

~*~

Jordan watched the wagon pull up in front of the doctor's office. They had to pass right by the building he lived in, though none of them knew that. Zach appeared wounded, shot in the back by the looks of his bloody shirt and Lily's bloody dress.

He watched out the window until Jake and his family came out, followed by Zach and Lily. She had her arm around Zach's waist, and he had his left arm around her shoulder. He appeared to be leaning on her a bit. He'd definitely been wounded. He was shirtless and his chest was bound in a bandage. She was careful to keep her hand at his waist and below the bandage.

Anger radiated through him. Who dared to try and steal away his pleasure again? Seeing them die — all of them — was his right.

He'd find out who did this and put an end to this folly. Shooting at Zach simply could not happen again. No one would take away the pleasure of killing Zach Anderson from him.

No one.

~*~

Lily managed to keep from crying in front of Zach. For him to know how scared she was for him wouldn't do. Or how much she cared. Caring for him wouldn't do her any good. She refused to love him. Refused to let him, or any man, hurt her again. That's all love was. A way for them to get you to put aside your defenses and then walk away when you were the most vulnerable. That's what Beauregard had done. She'd been sure she loved him, only to find out the feeling turned to hate rather quickly when he abandoned her. Then she found out she wasn't the only one he'd done it to.

Now she was sure he was the one who shot Zach. Sure that Jake was now letting Liam know that fact, too. She needed to see Beauregard and warn him to leave town. For his own sake, if he wanted to live. The problem was she didn't know where he was. The Grand Hotel was the best bet, though if he was running out of money, he might not be there anymore.

Lily wiped her eyes and regained her

composure. She went into the bedroom to check on Zach and found him sleeping with Daisy, the kitten, curled up next to him. The willow bark tea had done its job. The warm liquid concoction took away enough of his pain that he could sleep, at least for a little while.

She went out into the living room and took her shawl off the peg behind the door, put it on, and then slipped quietly out into the cool evening air. Walking quickly, she stepped over horse droppings, called road apples in these parts, along with cow pies, mud puddles, and numerous other forms of filth, to make her way up the street to the Grand Hotel. Once there she made her way across the foyer to the front desk where Mr. Farnum, the owner, stood.

"Is Beauregard Parkerson still registered here?"

"Yes, ma'am, Miss Sutter—"

"It's Mrs. Anderson, now, Mr. Farnum. Please continue."

"He's in room number eight and..." Mr. Farnum paused and cleared his throat, "he's indicated you would make good on his room bill."

Lily pulled herself to her full height of five foot two inches. "I most certainly will not. His hotel bill is his own. You'll have to take that matter up with him."

She whirled away and started up the stairs without waiting to hear what else Farnum had to say.

When she reached number eight she knocked lightly, then, thinking better of being lady-like, pounded on the door. "Beauregard Parkerson, you snake!" she hollered through the door. "You let me in this minute."

The door cracked open. "Be quiet would you. What do you want?"

"I want to talk," said Lily, pushing open the door and walking in.

The room was a disaster. It looked like a hurricane had hit it. Clothes were strewn everywhere. Beauregard moved the clothes that were in the single chair in the room and indicated she should sit.

She declined the gesture.

"You need to get out of town, Beauregard." She made the statement straightforward and without preamble. "Otherwise, you could die."

"Die? Why would I die?"

"Because you didn't kill Zach when you shot him and he's coming after you."

She saw the sweat start to roll down the side of his head.

"I...I didn't shoot him," he stuttered. "I...I was here when it happened."

"How would you know when it happened, if you didn't do it?"

"Well...I..." he blustered, tugging on his shirt collar.

"I'm only warning you because I don't want my husband to become a murderer."

"Husband!?"

His tone held no stuttering now, only anger.

He grabbed her by the arm. "How could you have married him? You loved me."

Frowning, she pulled her arm from his grasp. "Don't touch me. That love turned to hate a long time ago. Zach and I married this morning. This is your only warning. Get out of Deadwood, while you still can."

With those words, Lily turned and left the room without even looking back to see the effect they had. She'd done her good deed. She warned him. Whether he took her advice or not was up to him. He might not be able to leave town, now that Farnum knew he couldn't pay his bill. He might go to jail or have to work the bill off. Either way, he'd be stuck here. It would serve him right. Trying to kill Zach. The stupid man. Did he really think she'd fall back into his arms with Zach out of the picture? The only arms she'd fall into were Zach's.

She admitted she was beginning to care for him much more than she should. Husband or not, she wouldn't be put in the position of falling in love with Zach. She couldn't. Wouldn't. Her stomach did a flip when she thought of him. Ah, hell. She already had. She knew it as soon as she agreed to marry him. But she wouldn't admit it, not even to herself. Then when he got shot. She knew. No use lying to herself anymore. But she would not tell Zach.

He said he loved her, but what if that was just a ploy to get her to marry him. What if he was playing with her feelings like Beauregard did?

Don't be stupid, girl. Zach didn't have to marry you. He could have left you to figure out what to do about Beauregard without his help.

She shook her head. *No, I can't be vulnerable.*

I can't let down my guard. I have to be strong, for Gemma and for me. If I don't depend on anyone, I won't be hurt again.

CHAPTER 11

When Lily got back home, she took off her shawl, replaced it on the peg behind the door and then went to check on Zach. She found him awake.

"Where have you been?" he asked.

He didn't shout, but he was angry. She could tell. He didn't like for her to be gone.

"I went to see Mrs. Ferguson, like I told you I would." It wasn't a complete lie, she had stopped to see the woman on her way back from warning Beauregard.

She saw him relax back into the pillows.

"Oh, I forgot," he said, closing his eyes.

"How are you feeling?" She went to him and checked his forehead with the inside of her wrist. He was warm.

"I'm tired and I hurt. How do you think I'm feeling?"

"You're also cranky. I'll make you some more tea. It'll help."

She straightened to leave.

He grabbed her hand and held tight.

"I saw you go to the hotel," he whispered.

Oh, dear. What now? "What were you doing out of bed? Spying on me?"

"Why did you go to the hotel? To warn Parkerson?"

She pulled her hand out of his.

"Yes, as a matter of fact I did. I told him it was his only warning and if he wanted to live he'd better leave."

He frowned. "Why'd you warn him? Do you still love him?"

Her mouth fell open. How could he think for a moment that she still loved Beauregard?

"No, I don't still love him. I hate him. But I don't want to see you kill him. Some day he'll get on someone else's bad side and he'll get what's coming to him. But your hands will be clean."

His eyes narrowed and with the frown he looked quite menacing. "Why do you care so much about him?"

She closed her eyes and pinched her nose between them. "It's not him I care about, you dolt. It's you."

Opening her eyes, she saw him grinning. "I just wanted you to admit it. You care for me. That's a start, a good start, to loving me." His mouth tightened into a straight line. "You will love me someday. You know that, don't you?"

"No, I won't," she said softly. *I already do.*

~*~

Jordan nonchalantly climbed the stairs to number eight. He'd been watching the store, and he'd followed Lily on a hunch. This Parkerson fellow was Lily's old beau, he knew that for certain now. For some reason, she must feel she owed him. Why, Jordan didn't understand. The man had left her, pregnant and alone and now she thought she owed him.

Women. Except for watching them die, Jordan didn't have any use for the contrary creatures. Now, watching the light leave their eyes and the life leave their bodies, that was something to see. Something he craved. Something he'd experience with Lily, but in the meantime, he needed to rid himself of this Parkerson person. He was upsetting Jordan's plan, though he didn't know it. Regardless of whether he was aware of his mistake or not, Jordan would not let him interfere.

Jordan knocked on the door.

It opened immediately. "Come back to apologize?" said Parkerson as he opened the door.

"No. I don't think so," said Jordan. *He thinks I'm Lily or he's stupid enough to open the door to everyone.*

Parkerson's smile left his face. He backed into the room.

"I didn't mean anything by what I said. I just wanted Lily."

He started rambling, talking quickly, as though there was any explanation that would suffice. Jordan entered the room and closed the door behind him. He approached Parkerson. "I know you didn't. You don't even know my plans, now do you..." he paused.

"Beau. My name's Beau." The room wasn't very big and he stood stiff against the wall next to the bed. "That's right, mister. I don't know your plans."

"Let's just say, Beau, that I don't want Zach Anderson or Lily Sutter killed. At least, not yet."

Parkerson swallowed hard. "I'd never kill

Lily, but they're married now, so it wouldn't do me any good anyway. To have him dead. She'd still have his family to lean on and wouldn't need me." He shook his head and looked at the floor. "Wouldn't want me."

Jordan closed his eyes and took a deep breath. This man was more than just plain stupid. He was idiotic. "So your plan was to kill Anderson so Lily would come running to you?"

"Yes." He raised his chin.

"And you thought this because she had come running to you before?"

"Well, no, but I thought…"

Jordan grabbed Parkerson by the back of the neck and touched his forehead to Parkerson's.

"You didn't think. You didn't think at all."

Jordan pressed his knife just below the rib and shoved up into the heart. The death was quick.

Jordan held him and watched. Saw the knowledge of his death enter Parkerson's eyes, the shock, the resignation, and then, the finality. All those emotions in just a few seconds. The dimming light in their eyes was what Jordan waited for, what he wanted to see.

What he *craved*.

He wiped his knife on the bed sheet and then cleaned his hands in the basin of water that sat on the dresser. He checked his appearance in the mirror. Bowler hat, fake brown beard, and long wig. Three-piece black suit with white shirt and black tie. These theater people were proving to be a rich source of disguises. He could leave his room and not look the same way twice. He was becoming quite adept at applying the beards and mustaches, and the costumes provided him with clean clothes when he needed them. One of the benefits of living above the laundry was that the owner washed Jordan's clothes as part of the rent and his sheets were always clean. Satisfied with what he saw, he put on his black riding gloves and left the room.

~*~

Lily awoke to Zach thrashing and moaning. She'd been sleeping next to him, as they had agreed, since he was shot. She put her hand on his chest and tried to calm him.

"Zach. Zach! Wake up!"

He was burning up. An infection had set in, despite the doctors efforts by using the whisky in the wound.

Heart pounding, Lily got out of bed, poured water from the pitcher she kept on the dresser, into the basin next to it, and then soaked a washcloth in the cool liquid. She wrung it out and gently laid it on his forehead.

He immediately stopped thrashing and leaned into the wet cloth.

"Lily," he croaked. "So thirsty."

Of course. She got the glass off the nightstand and filled it with cool water.

"Here." With a hand under his neck, she angled his head and held the glass to his lips.

He drank greedily and she refilled the glass.

"I'm so hot," he complained.

"I know. I know you are. Let me cool you down." She put on her robe and then opened the window. The air was cool at night, even in July. When she came back to the bed, she took the cloth from his head and soaked it in the basin before wringing it out and wiping him down with it.

At each pass she made with the cloth she felt the heat coming off him in waves.

He shoved off all the covers and laid there in the nude, the breeze from the window cooling his overheated body. *When did he take off his underdrawers? He must have while she was at the hotel warning Beauregard.*

Lily checked the bandage and saw the seepage of blood.

"Zach, I need to change your bandage and clean your wound. You've got an infection. Can you sit up?"

He nodded and swung his legs over the side of the bed, then sat on the edge.

From around his chest she unwrapped the bandages and examined the wounds. The larger of the two wounds, the exit wound she knew from watching Doc Cochran sew them up, was oozing blood and puss. Her stomach clenched.

"I need to heat water and clean your wound. It's infected."

"Alright, do what you have to."

He wasn't delirious, which was a good thing, but he was sick.

"Lie back and I'll return as soon as I can."

She went into the kitchen, stoked the fire under one of the burners, and put a kettle of water on to boil. While the water heated she got the laudanum and put several drops in a glass of water and took it back to Zach.

"Here. Drink this to help with the pain."

He dutifully drank it all down. "That's disgusting."

"Do you want me to put sugar in it like I do for Gemma?"

"No." He shook his bent head. "I was just stating a fact, not asking you to fix it."

She laughed. "Glad to see you're still your grumpy self."

"I'm not grumpy. Gemma doesn't think I'm grumpy."

"Gemma loves you."

"And I love her," he responded without hesitation.

The walls around Lily's heart melted just a little more. With each passing day, she found it harder to keep from loving him. Or at least, admitting she loved him. She couldn't do that. Couldn't give in. Couldn't give up her hard-won independence.

Soon the kettle began to whistle. She brought it into the bedroom and poured the hot water into the basin with the cool water already in it, placing the hot kettle on the floor, so as not to damage the dresser. When she had it the temperature she wanted, she took the washcloth, wet it in the hot water and scrubbed it over her bar of lye soap. She cleaned his wound with the soapy cloth, rinsing again and again, until the puss was gone and only blood remained. Then she dried the wounds and re-bandaged him. By the time he'd endured her ministrations, he was exhausted and needed to lie back down.

"I'm sorry, Lily. Sorry I'm so useless."

"Don't be ridiculous. If it weren't for you, I'd still be worrying about Beauregard trying to take Gemma. And if it weren't for me, you wouldn't be in the predicament you're in now. You wouldn't have been shot. Now just lie back," she placed her hands on his shoulders and gently pushed. "and let me take care of you."

With an exhausted breath, he did.

She emptied the basin, filled it with clean, cool water and started wiping down his body with a clean cloth to cool him.

He groaned.

"This wasn't what I had in mind for the nights after our wedding. I'd hoped they'd be much more romantic."

"Shh. Just get better." She cupped his cheek for a moment. "That's all that matters now. We'll work the rest out later."

"Alright." His eyelids were closing and he

was fighting to keep them open. The laudanum was working.

Soon, he was asleep, but she continued to wipe down his body with the cool cloths, hoping the fever would soon break.

Lily shivered and her head popped up. She'd fallen asleep sitting in the chair next to the bed and now her back was killing her. Sometime during the night Zach had gotten under the blankets. His fever had broken, but now he had the chills. She got up, stretched, braced a hand against her aching lower back, walked to the window and closed it. Then she went to his old bedroom, gathered the blankets from the bed and brought them back to their bedroom. She covered him up with the extra blankets and then climbed in bed next to him.

The breeze from the window had chilled her, too. She tried to warm him, but he was so cold even the extra blankets didn't seem to help. She remembered when Gemma had been sick with fever and then the chills had followed. Doc Cochran told Lily to hold Gemma's naked body next to her own. The skin-to-skin contact made the heat from Lily's body warm Gemma like no blankets ever could.

Lily took off her robe and nightgown and crawled into the bed next to Zach. His body was so cold, his skin was as though he'd just climbed out of an icy river. She wrapped her arms around his chest and placed a leg over his, trying for as much body contact as she could get.

Zach groaned in his sleep. "Lily."

"Shh, sweetheart, I'm here. You'll be fine. Shh, go back to sleep."

He cuddled into her, shifting her body so her back was next to his chest and he wrapped his arms and legs around her, effectively caging her with his big body. It didn't matter. He was warming. His shivers were fewer and he was resting more comfortably. She relaxed into his embrace and fell asleep.

The sensation was the most delicious one. Her breast felt full and she felt the pull of pleasure straight to her groin. She squirmed.

Zach raised his head from her breast. "Ah. The lady awakes."

"What the hell do you think you're doing?" She pushed him away and raised the sheet to cover herself, tucking it safely under her arms.

"Enjoying the naked woman in my bed,

who also happens to be my wife. I live in the best of all possible worlds. Oh," he frowned and shook his head. "Don't hide from me. You have a lovely body, Lily. Even more lush than I had imagined, and I have a very good imagination. How do you do it? Make yourself appear less shapely than you are? Your dresses fit you perfectly and show off a nice figure, but you have a lavish figure."

Her face heated. "I bind my breasts with cloth so they don't stand out so much."

"Well your method works, but it can't be very comfortable. I want you to stop this binding. We'll buy you new clothes that fit you properly. I won't have my wife in pain for vanity's sake."

"Well, I guess the appearance doesn't matter anymore," she conceded. "I'm married now; I don't have to worry about the men being too forward. You'll take care of that. They won't want to cross you, and I'm sure you'll remind them should they forget."

Keeping the sheet tucked tightly, she leaned over and plucked her robe off the floor next to the bed where she'd dropped it the night before. As swiftly as she could, she dropped the sheet, slipped into the garment and out of bed.

Zach chuckled. "You can't hide from me forever, Lily."

He was obviously amused by her shenanigans. "I can try," she retorted and turned her back on him.

Suddenly, Zach was there, stopping her from leaving. He wrapped his arms around her.

"Don't leave. You've thoroughly seduced me, Lily. From the day I first saw you, I wanted you for my own. To be my wife. I adore you, Lily. Let me love you."

He was completely uncaring of his own nakedness. She closed her eyes and tried to shut out his words but she couldn't deny how her heart pounded. The same words she longed to hear, but was afraid to believe.

"I...I" she grasped for anything to put off the inevitable. "You're wounded. You'll open your wounds, and I don't want that to happen."

"Lily." He kissed her behind her ear and down the soft skin of her neck. "I'll be careful."

Unable to resist, she bent her neck giving him better access. His kisses felt so wonderful. Giving in and making love with him would be so easy. Then she remembered the pain of Beauregard rutting on top of her and the memory was like a bucket of ice water had been thrown on her.

"I'm not ready. You said you'd give me time. At least until your wound heals."

"Until the stitches come out," he countered, still stroking a hand the length of her arm. "And you continue to sleep next to me. Without your nightgown. If I can't make love to you, I at least want to hold you."

"Why?" she tried unsuccessfully to keep the plea out of her voice.

"Because, I love you. I'm willing to do whatever I need to in order to convince you of that. I want you to understand that making love is pleasurable, probably the greatest pleasure a person can have."

How can he be so wrong? "If you're a man, maybe, but certainly not if you're a woman."

"Lily—"

Bang! Bang! Bang!

The pounding on the door brought their conversation to a halt.

"That's probably your brothers wanting to see if I killed you yet. Cover up and I'll bring them back."

She went to the door, pasted a smile on her face and opened it a crack.

Her smile faltered as she faced a tall man with curly brown hair. "Sheriff? What can I do for you this morning?"

He took off his hat. "Can I come in Miss Sutter, er, I mean Mrs. Anderson?"

"Of course, please." She gathered her robe at her neck with her hand and grabbed her shawl with the other, quickly covering up, then stepped back and let him pass.

"I'd like to speak to you and Zach, if you don't mind."

"Not at all. He's awake. He was shot in the back, you know." She led the way to the bedroom.

"Yes, ma'am, I heard. That's sorta why I'm here."

They walked back to the bedroom where Zach was now propped up with pillows in the bed. Lily sat on the edge of the bed and the sheriff in the chair next to it.

"Good morning, sheriff, sorry I can't greet you properly."

"That's alright, Zach. I heard about your getting shot and that a man by the name of Beauregard Parkerson might be responsible."

His gaze shifted between her and Zach.

"Yeah, I figure he shot me, so what? I'll take care of it when I'm out of this bed."

"Someone already did," said the sheriff.

"He left town?" asked Lily, noticing the hopeful tone in her voice.

"No ma'am. Someone killed him."

Her hand flew to her mouth, "Oh, my God. That's not possible. I just saw him three days ago."

"Yes, ma'am. The day Zach was shot. The day you two got married."

"What are you saying, sheriff?" asked Zach.

"I did some checking and you, Mrs. Anderson, appear to be one of the last people to see this Parkerson person, alive."

CHAPTER 12

"You can't seriously think Lily killed him," said Zach, as he tried to sit straighter in bed.

"No. Calm yourself, Zach, or you'll bust some stitches," said the sheriff. "We know a man came to see Parkerson shortly after Mrs. Anderson did. Well-dressed man with long, dark hair and beard, black suit and tie, bowler hat. Ring a bell?"

Lily shook her head. "No one specific. I see most everyone who comes in to town at one time or another, but any number of men could fit that description."

"I know," said the sheriff with a nod. "That's my problem."

"Your suspect could be Richard Jordan,"

said Zach as he scratched his chin. "He has it out for me, but the last time he was seen, actually by Lily here, he was bald. I don't think he could grow his hair and beard in just a couple of weeks."

"Do either of you know who might have wanted Parkerson dead?"

"Anyone who met him," grumbled Zach, under his breath.

"No," said Lily and swatted Zach's arm. "Be serious."

"Oww. I am being serious. I can't imagine anyone who met him not wanting to kill him."

Lily rolled her eyes and pressed her lips tight.

The sheriff smiled as he stood. "Well, I'll let you two newlyweds be alone. Congratulations on your marriage."

"Thanks," said Lily and Zach together.

"I'll show you out," she said, recovering some of her good manners.

"No need." The sheriff waved her off. "I can find my own way."

He shook Zach's hand and nodded to Lily, before putting on his hat and leaving the room.

Lily worried her bottom lip and reminded herself to stop or it would chap. She hated that she was feeling a huge sense of relief. "Who do you think killed him?" Before Zach could respond with a smart remark, she held up her hand. "Seriously."

"I don't know," said Zach. "I was only half-joking when I said anyone who met him. Your old flame knew how to rub people the wrong way."

"He was also quite charming when he wanted to be. Just ask those other three young women he left in a family way like he did me."

Zach looked at Lily as she sat on his bed. Really looked at her. There was more to her than just the pretty blond woman wearing a flowered pink robe. He saw the vulnerable girl she'd been when Parkerson took advantage of her, and he saw the strong woman she'd become. She hadn't married for security, but chose instead to raise Gemma on her own.

He was well aware that if not for her fear of Parkerson, she wouldn't have married him now. But she wasn't running anymore and he was the best choice at hand for protecting Gemma.

Maybe he needed to give Lily something she couldn't get from any other man. Choice. She needed him and hadn't had much choice but to marry him when she did. But now, as her husband, he could give her the decision to make love or not. He needed her to know she was safe and for her to want to come to him. She was the one with the power.

Afraid of giving up her hard-won independence, she was bucking at everything. As far as Zach was concerned, she could keep her independence. Continue to run the store if she wanted, and he'd help her just like he was doing now. They'd work as partners in everything. Equal, if that was possible. He'd do his best to make it so. Anything that he could do to comfort Lily, make her love him, he'd do. But he knew in his heart she already loved him. No matter what, she wouldn't have married him, if she didn't. She wasn't that kind of woman.

He'd told himself he wouldn't tell her he loved her again until she admitted it to him, but his resolve flew out the window each time he saw her. He wanted her to know how he felt. Hell, he wanted the whole world to know. He took her hand brought it to his lips and kissed the palm, while he kept his gaze locked with hers.

Lily smiled but her brow wrinkled. "What

was that for?"

"To thank you and let you know how much I love you."

She turned away her head and stared at the floor. "Zach, don't. Don't say things like that."

"Lily, look at me."

When he saw she didn't move, he added, "Please."

Slowly, she turned her head blinking at tears in her big blue eyes.

"I will never lie to you. Ever." He stroked her cheek. "You can rely on me to at least tell you the truth, no matter what. I want there to be that between us, if there is nothing else. Truth. No lies. Not to each other or to ourselves. Do you agree?"

"Of course. I'd never lie to you—"

"No, I know you wouldn't, but I think you lie to yourself. You're afraid to let yourself love anyone, especially me."

She shook off his hand and jumped up from the bed. "You don't know me. You don't know anything. You don't know what it was like in the war, what I went through. I was a child, just sixteen."

He watched her, chest heaving in her anger

and all he could think of was how magnificent she was. If he wasn't wounded, and if every move he made didn't make him hurt, he'd gather her in his arms again and kiss her senseless. But that wasn't what she needed now and such an action wasn't what he needed either.

"Tell me. I want to understand. I was in the war too. I know things happened that shouldn't have. I'm sorry for that, but I didn't do them. When I could, I stopped them."

"If it hadn't been for Liam…"

"Liam?" Now he was thoroughly confused. "What does Liam have to do with this?"

She sank into the chair next to the bed and wrapped her arms around her waist. "He saved me."

"Saved you? In the war? You couldn't have been more than a child."

Her voice came softly, as though she was far away. "I was home, alone, with no one but the slaves when the soldiers came. I tried to hide, but two of them found me out by the barn. They laughed. Shoving me back and forth from one man to the other. Laughing while I screamed. They ripped my dress and were about to rape me when Liam came around the corner and saw what was happening. He ordered them to stop, and then put them to digging ditches for what they'd done."

He sat on the edge of the bed and reached to put his hands on her knees. "I'm so sorry, Lily."

"Liam saved me." She sniffled, took the handkerchief from her pocket, wiped her eyes and blew her nose. "He doesn't remember but I do. When Horace died and I had to sell the mine, I had the letter from Liam asking if there were mines for sale. Lots of people make inquires like that and I went through them and saw his. That was why I sold the mine to him, even though there were others that I could have sold it to sooner. I remembered his name and that he saved me. I wanted to pay him back."

"I'm glad he was there to help you. There were many others we couldn't help. I know this. I saw the aftermath, but we couldn't save everyone."

"For a long time I blamed every Yankee I saw. Then when Horace brought Gemma and me to Deadwood, I realized I couldn't do that if I was going to make a living. Little by little, since you Anderson's showed up, I've remembered that bad things happened on both sides. The South was not blameless."

"I don't know how you do it. How you could forgive…"

Her gaze snapped to his. "I don't forgive or forget, I just get on and remember that it was a Yankee who saved my life. I surely would have died that day, if not for Liam. I owed him."

Something awful occurred to him and his whole body tensed. "Is that why you agreed to marry me? Because you thought you owed Liam?"

"No!" She jumped up and paced to the window. "I would never do that. My debt to Liam was paid with the mine. As it turned out, more than paid, since you struck it rich."

"Part of that is yours now, too."

"Do you think I married you for the money?" She turned away from the window to face him. "Is that what you think of me? That I'm just another gold digger?"

"No." He shook his head. "I don't. But isn't that how you look at me, as just another man who's going to use you, and then walk away?"

He was yelling and he didn't care.

Her gaze ran his body from head to toe and stopped at his groin. He realized that he was standing there yelling at her buck naked. He didn't care.

"I don't think you'll walk away, and if you do, I've got your money to show for it."

"Don't count on it." His hands fisted. "I'll never walk away. I'm not Parkerson. I'm not those men who tried to rape you. I love you, damnit!"

"Put on your pants and get back in the damn bed," she yelled back. "You'll open your wound."

He watched her blue eyes flash fire. If he wasn't so angry, he'd kiss her. He grabbed his pants off the end of the bed and shoved his legs into them. "Better?" he shouted when he sat back on the bed.

"Yes." She closed her eyes and her chest heaved with exertion. "Yes, thank you," she said more softly.

"I'm sorry, Lily." He swallowed hard and closed his eyes. "I don't want us to fight."

She wrapped her arms back around her waist, in her protective stance, and nodded. "I don't want to fight either, but I won't be pushed or bullied."

"I don't want to push you or bully you. I want us to build on this marriage. Make it real. Make it work." He ran a hand through his hair. "I'm here for the long haul. I'm not leaving and not just because I'm wounded. I'm staying even if you throw me out. I'll be back every day. I won't walk away."

She thought for a long while before answering. "I'll try if you will. That's all I can promise right now."

"I will. Give me a chance to prove that I'm not like the others. I know you have some faith in me or you wouldn't have rented me Horace's room. You at least feel a modicum of safety around me."

"That's true," she admitted.

"Then let's build on that." He rose from the bed and walked over to her. Knowing she was wary and kissing her wouldn't be the right thing to do at this moment, he held out his hand. "Shake on it?"

She nodded and took his hand with hers. Her skin was so soft and he wanted nothing more than to pull her into his arms, but he resisted. Instead he held her hand for just a moment before he let go. "Good. How about some coffee since we're both up?"

"I'll get it started after I dress." She went behind the screen in the corner of the room and put on her clothes. He saw the frock she'd had on when he'd been wounded was ruined, soaked with his blood, and lay in a heap in the corner of the room.

"I'm sorry about your dress," he said pointing at the pile.

"It's nothing. My husband is a rich man and will buy me more." She grinned. Her levity eased the tension that had filled the room.

He chuckled. "You're right, he will. You order as many as you want. At least one for everyday and a couple of extra nice ones for church on Sunday."

She brightened. "I was kidding, Zach. You don't have to buy me dresses."

"I want my ladies dressed in style. After we catch Jordan and Gemma can come back home, I want new clothes for her, too."

Tears filled her eyes, and for a moment he thought she would cry, but she bent over and disappeared behind the screen. When she straightened, her eyes were clear. He thought maybe he imagined the whole thing.

She came out from behind the screen wearing the dress she'd worn yesterday. It was a nice green one with lace at the sleeves and the collar.

He could tell she hadn't bound her breasts because the bodice was straining at the buttons.

"We have to get you a new dress or two as soon as possible," he said looking at her chest.

She reddened.

He was immediately sorry he'd said anything. It wasn't his intention to embarrass her.

"I'll come back before we go out and dress properly, but I thought for now going without the binding would be fine."

"Of course, it is. I'm sorry, I shouldn't have said anything. We will take some time to get used to knowing what to say and what not to," he admitted.

"We already said we will be truthful with each other. You shouldn't have to know what to say. You can say anything to me." She walked ahead of him down the hall to the kitchen.

So he couldn't see her face now, but in her voice he heard the embarrassment. "I should still have some tact and I didn't, for that I apologize. Let's get that coffee and breakfast. Then we can drive out to Liam's and see Gemma."

"And let them know what happened," she said finishing his thought.

"Yes. I believe Jordan may have been who killed Parkerson because Parkerson shot me." He leaned in the doorway of the kitchen, arms crossed over his chest, while she started breakfast. "Jordan wouldn't want anyone to interfere with his plans. He's a meticulous planner and he is very upset when things don't go his way. That's what started him after us to begin with."

She got the coffee started and put a skillet on another of the burners to heat while she pulled bacon from the icebox. Lily put four slices of bacon across the bottom of the pan.

Zach could hear it start to sizzle. His stomach growled in response.

"You must be hungry," she said at the gurgling sound his stomach made. "It's understandable. You haven't really eaten for three days. Hot soup and willow bark tea don't count."

"I am hungry," he said rubbing a hand

over his bare stomach. Realizing for the first time that he'd only put his pants on, he said, "Excuse me while I get a shirt."

"Don't dress on my account," she said as he left the room.

He heard a small chuckle, then her voice louder, "Be careful and don't open your stitches." He was half way across the parlor when he turned and answered.

"I won't." He went to the closet in his old bedroom and pulled a black shirt off a hanger. If he did happen to bleed through, it wouldn't show against the black of the shirt.

An hour later they'd finished breakfast and were on their way, walking to Jake's to borrow his buckboard.

"I'm so excited to see Gemma," said Lily.

Zach could see the excitement shining in her eyes.

"She and I haven't ever been apart for more than a night. This has been difficult. I hope she's okay."

Zach took Lily's hand in his and gave it a squeeze. "I'm sure she's been fine. Having Hannah there to play with has been a great treat for both of them."

"I know. Gemma gets lonely with just me

for company. She loves going to school and being with the other kids. Do you think she'll have to stay at Liam's for very much longer?"

"Probably, but I know you miss her and we'll try to get up to see her more often. I'll ask Liam to bring her down on Sundays, too. I still think she should stay with him. She's safer there."

They reached Jake's house and Zach knocked on the door.

"Zach," said Jake when he opened the door. "What are you doing here and why aren't you in bed?"

"I could say the same thing to you. What are you doing home? Why aren't you at the mine?"

"I've been working on the house, trying to get it finished inside the way I want it. Besides, Liam has everything covered at the mine and he's close if they need him on site."

"I've got things to do, too," said Zach. "I can't stay in bed all the time. I'll just try to take it a little easy but now I want to borrow your buckboard so we can go see Gemma."

"Of course. Let me hitch it up. You may be up and around but that doesn't mean you should be doing any heavy lifting."

"I won't argue with you. I've already been warned not to bust my stitches," he said winking at Lily.

"That's right," she confirmed, ignoring his wink. "I don't want Doc to have to redo the fine work he did."

They all started laughing knowing Doc Cochran only put as much effort into his stitches as he had to. There was nothing pretty or neat about them. They served a function, that was all.

"When do you get them out?" asked Jake as they walked to the stable behind his house.

"Not for another ten days or so, I guess. I haven't exactly been myself lately, so I don't really know." He leaned against the wall of the stable, finding himself a little shaky at the moment, though he wouldn't let them know. "Lily's been taking care of me."

"He got a fever and infection despite Doc's efforts. Then he got the chills," said Lily, frowning.

"That happened to me after I got wounded," said Jake. "Becky had to warm me with her body, I was so cold."

Lily felt the heat rise up her neck. She was embarrassed to her toes that Jake might guess she'd been naked with Zach.

"We have some news for you."

Lily looked over at him and mouthed "Thank you."

"What's that?" asked Jake, setting the harness on the horses back and tightening the girth.

"Someone killed Beauregard Parkerson, Lily's old beau. I think he's the one who shot me and I intended to do something about that when I recovered but someone beat me to it."

"He wouldn't have killed him," Lily added quickly with a shake of her head.

Jake and Zach looked at each other, both knowing the truth. If it came down to it and Zach was given no choice, he'd have killed Parkerson in a heartbeat. Neither of the men said anything.

"So you're driving to Liam's to see Gemma?" asked Jake.

Before Lily got an education on the law of the west, Zach said, "Yes, we miss her." He didn't miss the look of surprise on Lily's face at his words. But they were true. He did miss the little moppet.

"Are you sure you're well enough to drive the buckboard?" asked Jake.

"If he can't, I'm fully capable. I drove around our plantation all the time as a child, much to the disappointment of my mother and the delight of my father, who was perfectly happy as long as I was irritating my mother." She smiled and then leaned forward and talked behind a hand at the side of her mouth. "They didn't get along too well."

Jake chuckled and then helped first Lily, and then Zach up to the bench.

Zach was already weak as a kitten from the little exertion the walk over had given him.

"We don't have to do this today. You should be in bed. You're white as a sheet," said Lily, touching the inside of her wrist to his forehead. "At least you don't have a fever."

"No. I'm fine," insisted Zach. "I want to see Gemma, and we need to talk to Liam."

"Well, I'm driving. I'm afraid you'll fall off the bench and take the reins with you, you're so weak."

"Ha." He snorted, then all bravado aside he said, "I wouldn't mind if you do. I do believe you're right and I've pushed my ability to the limit, but I need to see Liam. It's important."

"Zach, getting you well, is important," said

Lily, snippily. Then more gently, "I'm not ready to be a widow."

He laid his hand on her knee. "I'm not ready to make you one. Let's hurry to Liam's so we can get back home."

Compared with the last time they tried to go to Liam's, this trip was positively peaceful. Once they arrived, Lily got down from the wagon by herself and then walked around to help Zach.

"I'm too big for you, you better get Liam. I'll need his help."

Lily ran to the house and was met there by Liam who had the door wide open.

"Lily, come in. What—"

"He needs you." She turned and ran back to the buckboard with Liam hot on her heels.

"Zach, what the hell are you doing?" Liam reached up and helped his brother down. Then he put Zach's good arm around his neck and assisted him into the house, taking slow steps.

"I needed to see you and—"

"Mommy! Zach!" Gemma ran at them from the hallway that led to the bedrooms, Hannah right behind her.

With a gasp, Lily bent down and caught her daughter just as she launched herself into

Lily's arms.

"Gemma. Baby. Mommy's missed you so much." Lily hugged her small body tight almost afraid to let her go. Her little girl scent wafted to Lily's nostrils and she inhaled deeply.

"I've missed you, too. I've had lots of fun with Hannah. But I'm ready to go home and see Daisy."

The kitten missed Gemma, too, thought Lily. She'd taken to sleeping on Gemma's pillow.

Zach and Lily sat on the sofa in front of the fireplace. She held Gemma on her lap. "Oh, baby, I want more than anything for you to come home. Zach is your new daddy now. He and mommy got married, did I tell you that before? No, of course, I haven't. I haven't seen you since it happened."

Gemma rested her head on her mother's shoulder and reached over and patted Zach's hand. "Mr. Anderson told me. He said I might have to stay here longer, 'cause I need to be safe." She looked up at Lily. "Can't I be safe with you?"

Cornflower blue eyes the exact same shade as Lily's own, looked up at her. "Baby, you will be, but not until Zach is well."

Gemma's gaze snapped to Zach's. "Are you sick?"

"Don't worry, sweetie, I'll be fine."

Lily looked at him and saw his color was returning. With a little more rest here, the trip back to Jake's shouldn't be too bad but the walk back to the mercantile would again sap his strength. Worry attached her thoughts as she stroked Gemma's hair.

"No, sweetheart, Zach's wounded. A very bad man shot him and he's got to heal before you come home."

"It's all right," said Zach, reaching out then, wrapping the little girl in his arms. Lily saw the grimace that fleetingly crossed his face but he said nothing, simply hugged Gemma close.

"Can I call you Daddy?"

"If you want to, I'd be very pleased."

"Good," she said and leaned against his chest.

"Are you happy I married your mama?"

Gemma nodded ferociously. "Maybe then you'll have a baby like Hannah's mommy and daddy are, then I'll have my own little sister to play with."

Zach looked up at Liam and cocked an eyebrow.

Liam looked a little sheepish. "I guess we all have some news to share." He grabbed Ellie around the waist and brought her close. "Doc Cochran just confirmed it."

Lily leapt up, eased Liam out of the way and hugged Ellie. "I'm so happy for you."

"We're thrilled," giggled Ellie. Happiness radiated from her.

Lily could see the bloom of roses on the tall brunettes face. The old wives tale was true, pregnant women glowed. Ellie could be a plain woman to some people's way of thinking, but she'd always been beautiful to Liam. The more Lily got to know her, the more she felt the same way. Ellie had a beauty that wasn't typical, but was there nonetheless.

"And you, too," said Lily to Liam. "Congratulations."

Liam's chest pushed out. "Thank you." He shoved his thumbs in his pockets. "We're all really pleased. Hannah's probably the most excited. She's never been a big sister before. David is hoping it's a boy. Ellie and I don't care as long as the babe is healthy." He leaned in and spoke quietly. "I'm a little worried because this is Ellie's first baby, but she says she'll be fine."

"And I will be," confirmed Ellie with a short nod. "Doc says if I follow his instructions, I should be fine, even though I'm so old."

"You're not old," Liam, Zach, and Lily said together like a chorus.

"I'm old to be having a first baby. By the time the child is born I'll be thirty-three." She smoothed the front of her bluse, her hands lingering over her belly.

"That's not old," insisted Lily.

"You're sweet, and now you're my sister-in-law. It's so marvelous. It was just Father and me for so long, but now, I've got all this family and they're all deluded, but I don't mind."

Lily glanced at Zach and noticed him wince while holding Gemma.

"Zach," she spoke in a quiet tone.

He looked up at her where she stood next to Ellie. "Yes."

"Can I see you privately, please? Ellie, can we borrow your bedroom?"

"Sure. Gemma, you and Hannah go outside and play."

She slid off his lap. The two little girls

giggled and ran outside.

Zach swung his gaze to hers, eyebrows winging high.

"Don't get excited," she said to Zach, then to Ellie, "I need to check Zach's wound. In the mean-time could you start some water for willow bark tea?"

"It's on the stove, hot. I'll start the tea to steeping," said Ellie. "Let me know if you need anything else."

Lily waved at his chest. "Go ahead and take off your shirt. There's no need to go to the bedroom since the girls are outside."

Zach unbuttoned his shirt and winced when he tried to slip it off his shoulders.

Lily reached up and eased the shirt down his arms. "You're bleeding again. I knew you shouldn't have come today."

"I couldn't let you come by yourself. What kind of husband would I be?"

"A live one, because I will kill you."

Ellie giggled and Liam chuckled.

"I've got bandages and salve. Come to the kitchen and we'll get you all fixed up, Zach," said Ellie.

"I'll do it," said Lily. "Just put the supplies out on the counter, please."

"Surely," answered Ellie with a smirk.

Lily and Zach followed Ellie to the kitchen with Liam bringing up the rear. Ellie went into the pantry and brought out a stack of white cloth bandages, a nasty smelling salve, and wash cloths, then got the basin from under the sink. She took a cup, put a measure of dried herbs into it and poured water over the top. Next, she placed the cup on the table in front of Zach.

Lily poured hot water from the kettle into the basin and then poured in some cold from the pump at the sink. She added soap chips and rinsed the cloth off in the hot water.

Once she cleaned away all the blood, she could see that the wound wasn't bad. He'd pulled a couple of stitches and was seeping steadily. She dried off the sore and applied the salve Ellie supplied. It stunk to high heaven.

"What is this stuff?" asked Lily.

"Horse liniment," said Liam.

"I noticed that you didn't flinch at the sight of it so you must have used it before. Have you?" she asked Zach.

"Yeah. The liniment helps heal and keep dirt out of the wound."

Lily leaned down to where Zach sat in the

chair at the kitchen table and whispered in his ear. "If you smell like this on a regular basis, you'll be sleeping by yourself."

He grinned up at her teasing. "I won't darlin' I promise. Nothing is going to keep me from sleeping with my lovely bride."

Lily knew she had the good grace to blush.

Liam cleared his throat. "Come on, Ellie. They don't need us now."

Ellie chuckled and followed Liam out of the kitchen.

"I'm a sorry excuse for a husband."

"No, you're not. We've just had a tough time lately. Not too many grooms get shot on their wedding day. You've had a bit of a rough start and our argument this morning didn't help." She cupped his cheek. "I'm sorry for that."

"Don't be," he said, holding his arms straight out so she could wrap him up again. "We got the air cleared, and we'll start over."

"Yes, we will, beginning now." Lily remembered the look of contentment on her daughters face while she was in Zach's arms. Could Lily find that same happiness if she let herself? She had to admit her heart lightened when she realized just how much Gemma loved Zach. She's ready to accept him as her father. Craved it even.

They went back out to the parlor where Liam and Ellie waited.

"So what gets you out of your sick bed and onto my doorstep this lovely day. And don't say you just wanted an outing."

"I think that Jordan is the one who killed Parkerson. I believe he was angry that Parkerson might have killed me and Jordan wouldn't get the chance."

"That makes sense," said Liam. "Based on what we know about Jordan, he doesn't like his plans upset."

The men cussed and discussed Jordan and two hours later, Zach was feeling better. Lily pronounced him ready to travel again. Liam helped them both up onto the wagon bench.

"Rest, Zach," said Liam. "If you have something you need from me, send word with Jake. I'll also have one of our men stop by every day and see if you need anything. You can give him a letter, at least until you get your stitches out."

"Alright," nodded Zach. "I'll follow the Doc's orders and stay in bed."

The trip back to town went too quickly. He

and Lily talked. Really talked.

"What do you want from our marriage?" asked Zach.

"I want children. I love children," said Lily, the tone in her voice a dreamy one. "And I want to continue running the mercantile. I like helping people, talking to them, learning about their lives."

"We don't need to do that. We have enough money, neither of us ever have to work again."

"But think how boring that would be. Don't you and your brothers miss working?"

"Liam wants us to open a bank. After what you've been through with Sam Toliver, I think it's a good idea. What do you think?"

"I think it's a wonderful idea. It would give you each something to do."

"I intend to continue helping you in the mercantile, if that's what you want to do."

"You'd do that for me?"

He nodded. "Of course. I want to spend as much time with you as I can. I'm not young and we have a lot of time to make up for."

"You're not old either. You're only thirty-eight, ten years older than me. That's not much."

He took her right hand and kissed it, while she held the reins with her left.

"What I want most of all is for Gemma to be happy and safe."

When Lily heard that, she felt her heart give way, she knew she could trust him completely. When he was better, she'd tell him. In the mean time she would use the time he gave her to get used to him. To learn him. She was a curious woman, fiercely independent and she would not be kept in the dark about anything, including what goes on between a man and a woman.

CHAPTER 13

Lily wanted to drop Zach off at the mercantile and she would take the wagon back to Jake's by herself, but Zach would hear none of her suggestion. So by the time they got back home, he was so worn out, Lily had to help him undress.

"You did too much today, but at least you're not bleeding again. Looks like that nasty-smelling salve is working."

"I am tired. Come lay with me." He patted the mattress next to him. "Just until I go to sleep."

She wanted to say no. Her ingrained responses were the first to rise, but she remembered Gemma's face. "Alright. First, let me make you some willow bark tea."

"No, I don't need any. I can handle it."

"I want to keep ahead of the pain. Choose either the tea or laudanum."

"I'll take the tea. At least it doesn't make me feel stupid. I still have all my thinking skills with the tea."

She bent over to tuck the covers around him so he didn't get chills again.

H reached up and ran a knuckle down her cheek.

"So soft. So beautiful."

"You're tired." She started to turn..

"That doesn't mean I don't know what I'm saying."

His words stopped her and she looked toward the bed.

"You have the softest skin I've ever felt, except for Gemma's. Her skin is just like satin. Yours is like silk. Both soft, both beautiful. I'm a lucky man, Lily, and I know it. I have two beautiful girls, that I adore and care about. One of whom already loves me and the other will come around."

Then he smiled and winked.

Winked. Those cobalt blue eyes hiding nothing.

She started laughing. "You're incorrigible, Zach Anderson. Completely and unabashedly.

I don't know why Gemma loves you so."

He gazed up at her. "Because she knows that I love her back, and I will always protect and love her. I'm thrilled she wants to call me 'Daddy'."

She got a lump in her throat. "She's never wanted to do that with anyone. Even when Horace was helping to raise her, she never once asked to call him 'Daddy' even though the other children often had fathers. Only you."

"I'm flattered beyond words." He smiled and touched her cheek.

"You should be. Now let me get your tea." When he started to protest, she added, "then I'll lie down beside you."

"Naked."

"Dressed."

"Naked," he insisted, grinning.

She shook her head. "In my nightgown, and that's as far as I'll go. Otherwise I'll sleep in the other room."

Pouting, he said, "Alright. I'd rather have you beside me with clothes on than not with me at all. But I warn you, when I'm better I plan on getting you naked."

"If you're very nice and really lucky, you

may get your way." She smiled, turned and left to get his tea.

Zach lay there, happiness warring with fatigue. He was glad they'd gone to Liam's, even though the trip tired him mightily. He'd reached a turning point with Lily. Something happened, and she was more open to his sensual advances. If he'd been healthy, and she'd been willing, he'd have made love to her until she screamed with delight. As it was, he'd have to wait.

Waiting would nearly kill him, he wanted her so much, but he wanted her first time to be wonderful. He realized the coupling wasn't her first time having sex, but it would be her first time making love and the union should be something she would remember fondly. He wanted their lovemaking to erase all her memories of everything that happened before. He wanted the experience to be perfect for her. Zach already knew it would be perfect for him.

He felt his eyes closing and was only vaguely aware of Lily joining him in the bed. Yet, he was drawn to her like a moth to the flame. He reached over and pulled her against him, felt her body relax against his. Contentment filled him as his fight with sleep was lost.

~*~

Ten days had passed since he'd relieved Mr. Parkerson of his life. Staying in this little room was boring and refraining from killing was hard. He liked the pleasure he felt from the deadly activity, too much. But resist he must. He didn't want to give himself away. Yet. They wouldn't know the hunter was him until it was too late to do anything. He'd come to realize killing them one at a time was going to be difficult. He may have to settle, for one. Just one of the Andersons, but which one?

Liam had surrounded himself with hired men and he'd taken the little girl, Gemma, into his household. There was no way he could get through those defenses.

Jake, though at the forefront of the original crime against Jordan, was too strong and he, too, had help. People in his house all the time. Cleaners, builders. Jordan had even thought of trying to pass himself off as one of the workers. But Jake had seen him in Missouri. It was Jake's fiancée Jordan had killed. His woman that Jordan had been denied the pleasure of watching her die. He would have done it anyway, make no mistake, but he would have killed her slowly, not shot her in the chest. He'd enjoyed no pleasure in that. The killing was just expedient.

Jake's fiancée was the cause of all this. If they had only been complete. If only he'd been able to leave before Jake saw him. If only Zach didn't know what he looked like. But Zach, especially, knew too much. He'd served under Jordan, knew his habits, at least the ones that the army valued.

So far he'd kept hidden enough to move among them on occasion, but he hadn't run into Zach one on one. Now was the time to strike, while he was still weak.

Jordan kept watch on the mercantile. He knew when Zach was alone, and once Zach was gone, he would enjoy Lily before he dispatched her to join her new husband.

He smiled.

~*~

Since she started sleeping with Zach, Lily awoke with the same lovely feeling every morning. It didn't matter what kind of nightgown she wore to bed, by morning, she would be naked to the waist and Zach's mouth doing absolutely lovely things to her nipples.

While his mouth sucked, nipped and laved

her right nipple, his hand rolled and pinched the other one. She'd wake up moaning, wanting more but he didn't press her, and until now she hadn't asked.

"Oh, God, Zach," she groaned. "How can you make me feel these things? I want so much more. I want to feel more."

"I can do that, if you're sure you're ready. Nothing would make me happier Lily, than to make love to you." He paused, looked her directly in the eyes. "Are you sure?"

Gazing into his cobalt blue eyes, Lily did her best to control her breathing and not pant, but excitement and need made her breathless. "Yes, Zach, I'm sure. I want to know…to feel. I want to have new memories. I don't deny I'm scared. But I trust you."

He smiled. "Those three little words are the second most important ones you can say to me. I'm humbled by your trust and I won't let you down. I promise."

He kissed her softly on the lips. Then moved to her chin and around her jaw to behind her ear and down the sensitive skin of her neck. Across her chest and down to her breast, he moved. Kissing all the way and stopping only to lave attention on her nipple that felt bereft after his attention from before. Wherever his lips touched, he left fire. She felt the blaze he left as he kissed all the way down her body.

"Zach, please."

He lifted his head and chuckled. "Your wish is my command."

He kissed her stomach, ran his tongue around and then stabbed it in and out of her belly button in a surprisingly erotic motion she knew he'd soon be doing with another part of his body.

Moving lower, he stopped, raised his head and looked at her.

"Lily, you have all the power. If you want me to stop, just—"

She grabbed handfuls of the sheets. "Will you shut up and get on with it."

"Your wish is my command." With those words he delved between her legs and suckled a spot that was so sensitive she nearly came off the bed. He held her down with his head and continued to lick. Around and around, then he'd stab it with the very tip of his tongue, then circle, suckle, and stab. Again and again until she thought she'd die from the wanting.

Then he pushed one finger into her body.

"God, you're so tight. I don't want to hurt you, Lily."

He was gentle and pumped his finger in and out until she was moaning with need. Then he placed a second and third finger inside, stretching her for his entry.

He worked her, suckling, gently scraping with his teeth, circling with his tongue, stabbing and suckling again. The rhythm, as old as time, pounded through her, singing through her body, making her crazy with need. She could barely stand it. Pressure built until she thought she'd explode and then…

"Oh, God, yes!" she shouted. She lifted off the bed and shoved her body against Zach's wonderful, talented mouth, greedy for all he could give her. He kept with her, gently laving, licking her until she relaxed, panting, in a heap on the bed.

She was limp. Sweat covered her body and she didn't care. The experience was the most amazing next to childbirth she'd ever had, and while that was pain, this was nothing but pleasure.

Zach kissed his way back up her body to her mouth and kissed her soundly.

"I'm going to make love to you now, Lily."

With those words he inched his shaft into her. She was slick and though he was large, there was no pain as there had been with Beauregard. He slid in easily, filling her completely. Then he stopped and held still.

"Zach?"

"Yes," he croaked.

"Are you done?"

"Hell no. Are you all right? Are you having any pain?"

"Hell no," she answered in imitation of his words.

"Thank God." He pulled back, nearly out of her, then pushed forward, harder and harder. In and out.

In short order, she found her own rhythm. Pulling back when he did, then forward. Each slam of their bodies together hit that wonderful spot Zach had worked on before and with each move, the delicious pressure built. Finally, she could stand no more. "Please, Zach, please."

He didn't answer, seemingly beyond speech, but he reached between them, rubbed her nub and slammed his body harder and harder against hers. Then he pumped one last time, gave a shout and she broke, scattered to the wind.

Zach collapsed on her, burying his face in the soft skin between her neck and shoulder, breathing hard.

She held him to her, enjoying the feel of his weight upon her and his member slowly retreating from her body.

For a long time, she didn't say anything.

"Lily?"

She heard the worry in his voice.

"Thank you." Those two words were all she could think of to say, but they were enough.

He rolled off of her to his side and brought her with him, spooning his body around hers.

"You're magnificent. Everything I knew you would be," he whispered in her ear.

"Will we do that often?"

"As often as we can, God willing, and that we have the strength for."

"Good," she said. She felt drowsy and complete for the first time in her life. Tomorrow she would tell Zach how she felt.

~*~

The next day Zach walked across town to Doc Cochran's office and had his stitches removed.

"The wounds look great. I should have thought of horse liniment myself. The salve works wonders on horses, no reason it wouldn't work on people."

"Thanks, Doc." He looked at the wound and saw the red, puckered skin and thought how the outcome could have been much worse. Luck was with him that day. The day he married Lily. He smiled.

"You seem particularly chipper today and I don't think it's from my prognosis." Doc cocked his head to the side. "Care to elaborate?"

"No, sir. I just discovered I'm sure my wife loves me."

"That's always a good thing to know," said Doc with a chuckle.

"Am I cleared to get back to regular livin', Doc?"

"Sure are. No need to worry about those holes. They are good as healed. I'd be prepared for some fatigue the first week or so while you get back into your normal routine. After that you should be fine."

"Great. I'll be careful. I surely don't want to see you again, at least on a professional level."

Both men laughed.

Zach shook Doc's hand. "Thanks for everything."

He walked back to the mercantile, a lightness to his step. The sky was clear and the air fresh. He and Lily would have a real marriage, he hoped a good one with lots of blue-eyed babies.

When he reached the store, he saw the door standing wide open, something Lily never allowed because she hated all the flies it let in. A frisson of fear snaked up his spine.

"Lily...Lily," he called as entered the store. He slowly looked down every aisle, behind every shelf. The store was empty. Heart pounding, he bolted to the back and up the stairs to their home. He slammed through the door. "Lily," he called. Silence.

No! She can't be gone. He ran through each room, ending with Gemma's. There he found her, sprawled unconscious on the bed, bruises forming on her eye and jaw. Her cheeks swollen and her beautiful lips split.

"Lily." He gently lifted her into his arms and carried her to their bedroom. He went to the kitchen and chipped ice from the big block in the icebox, wrapped it in a washcloth and laid it on her eye.

At the contact, she winced and opened her eyes, then flinched until she realized it was Zach.

He wanted to kiss her, hold her and let her know it was all right. She was safe. But now he needed to know what happened while the event was fresh in her mind. "What happened, love?"

"*He* came." Her eyes widened and he saw the fear. "I didn't recognize him at first. He's wearing an ugly red wig and fake beard. They're good. They look real until you're up close. Then you can tell it's a wig, but the beard definitely looked real, until I pulled some of the beard off." She opened her hand.

He glanced down and saw the red whiskers held there.

"He hit you." His voice was soft, deadly. He tried to keep out the menace for her sake but could not. He'd kill Jordan for this. "How did this happen?"

"He came into the store and I turned, smiled and asked 'Can I help you?' Just like I would any customer." Her eyes widened and she reached for Zach's hand. "He smiled back, and started walking toward me. That's when I saw the knife in his hand and I ran. I pounded up the stairs and screamed the whole time I was doing it. He chased me and finally caught me. He kept hitting me, telling me to shut up and finally I did. I passed out."

Why didn't he kill you? "I'm so glad he didn't use the knife."

She shook her head and winced at the motion. "I don't know why he didn't but I guess someone would notice if he had an unconscious woman slung over his shoulder."

Zach nodded, stroking her arm. That had to be it. Jordan didn't want any witnesses.

"Can you remember anything else about him? Anything that might help me to find him."

She shook her head and then looked up at him. "He smelled."

"Smelled?"

"Yes. Strongly. Of garlic."

"Garlic? That's the Celestials part of town. He's near someplace that cooks with lots of garlic. That helps a lot. I'm closing the store and taking you to Doc Cochran's to make sure nothing is broken. Then you're going to Jake's. You'll be safer there."

"I want to go with you—"

"No." He shook his head.

"—but I know I can't. You'd be worried about me and wouldn't be able to concentrate on finding him."

"That's right. Jake and I need to have our wits about us and we can't if we're worrying about you and Becky. Workers are always at Jake's house. I'll hire them to stop working and just guard you and Becky until Jake and I return."

She nodded, but fat tears rolled down her cheeks.

"Don't cry, love." He held her against his chest and smoothed his hand up and down her back. "Please don't cry."

She pulled back. "Why not? I've just found you. Found the love of my life and the man I want to father my babies and you're leaving and will possibly get yourself killed."

Zach started forming a plan. "I'm not going to get killed…what did you say?" He narrowed his gaze on her face.

"Possibly get yourself killed."

"Before that."

"Leaving."

He shook his head. "No, before that."

Suddenly, she smiled. "Oww." She gently

touched her split lip. "I've found the love of my life and the man I want to father my babies."

"Yeah, that's the part." Elated, he leaned down and kissed her very gently, aware that her lips had to be sore.

"Oh, Zach, you've been so patient with me. I was so afraid."

"Given your experiences, that's understandable."

"I don't want to be afraid anymore."

He smiled. He was so proud of her. She was taking control of her life. After being through one of the scariest experiences anyone, man or woman, could have, she was bouncing back. Determined. Strong.

"I love you, too, and I'm not letting anything happen to me, especially now that we have so much to look forward to."

They walked to Doc's. Zach was vigilant, looking around for the red-headed man Lily described, but he didn't see him. Arriving at their destination, he rapped on the door.

"Zach, Lily, my God girl, what happened?"

Doc showed them to his examination table. He looked over Lily, felt her jaws and probed, pressing his fingers against her face.

Zach told Doc about Jordan while Doc took care of Lily.

"I don't think anything is broken," said Doc, putting his stethoscope away. "But you're going to be black and blue for a few weeks. It's not going to be pretty."

"She's always beautiful to me, but I'll get Jordan and repay him in kind for this."

Lily squeezed his hand and gazed up at him from the table where she now sat. "Please be careful."

"Always," he brought her hand to his lips and kissed it.

They left Doc's and walked to Jake's house. Zach kept his vigilance up, not relaxing until he reached his brother's home.

Jake answered Zach's knock.

"Hi, brother, come on in."

They followed Jake into the living room where Becky sat on the sofa playing with Jenny.

"Oh, let me have that sweet baby," said Lily holding out her arms for the child.

"Lily, what the hell happened to your face?" asked Jake, as he sat back in his big brown leather chair.

Zach sat next to Lily on the sofa with Becky. "That's what we're here about," His frustration building, he ran his hands through his hair. He wanted to kill someone. He wanted to kill Jordan. Now. But he sat there, put his hand on Lily's knee and tried to remain civilized. "Jordan did this. I'm hunting down the bastard and killing him, like the animal he is. Do you want to come?"

"Hell, yes. I owe him." Jake turned to Becky and held his hand out until she grasped it. "You know I have to do this."

"I know," Becky said quietly. "We knew this day would come. I want you to get him. He can't be allowed to go on killing."

Lily held the baby close, as if she could shelter the little one from the ugliness her father and uncle were going to undertake.

"Lily said he smelled like garlic. You know what that means?" said Zach.

Jake nodded. "He's in Chinatown. They like to cook with garlic."

"Right. And if he smells that strongly, he not only lives near where it's being cooked, he's eating it, too."

"We should look for places around the restaurants and food stands where he could be living. Some cheap rooms are rented to white folks, but and this is good for us, there aren't that many."

A knock on the door sounded.

"I'll be right back," said Jake.

He returned a few minutes later with Liam following him.

"Well, looks like I missed the party," said Liam with a smile.

"Actually," said Zach, "you're right on time." He explained what he and Jake were about to do.

"I am just in time. I brought two men with me, I planned to station them at the mercantile. I know you haven't wanted them there, but I was going to anyway. I want you and Lily…what happened to you?" he said just noticing Lily's bruised face. His gaze flashed to his brother.

"Jordan," said Zach.

"Guess I should have put the men there sooner. I'm sorry, Lily."

"Don't be, Liam, the fault isn't yours. The man is a menace and he has to be stopped."

"I'm going with you," said Liam, jamming his hands on his hips. "With the three of us together, we should be able to stop him from hurting anyone else,"

"So what are you doing, exactly?" asked Lily.

"They're going to kill the scum," said Becky. "Don't be naïve and think they'll turn him over to the sheriff. It's gone way beyond that. It was already beyond that when he killed Elizabeth."

"Who is Elizabeth?" Lily bounced baby Jenny on her knee and cooed at her.

Zach loved seeing her with the baby. Imagining Jenny was their baby was easy and the thought warmed his heart. Yet daydreaming was something he didn't need now. He needed to stay cold blooded and get this deed done. He looked away.

"She was my fiancée," said Jake. "Jordan killed her in cold blood after his accomplice, who happened to be her ex-fiancé, had raped her."

His voice was flat, thought Zach, just like it had been the night he told Liam about it, more than a year ago.

Lily's hand flew to her mouth and she hugged baby Jenny even tighter. So much so, the baby began to fuss.

"Hush, now. Auntie Lily is sorry for

squeezing you." She soothed the baby and Jenny went back to sucking her fist. Lily looked over at Jake. "I'm so sorry for your loss, but I'm glad that you found Becky and moved on. I've learned it's something we all have to do if we're to be happy."

Zach took Lily's free hand, brought it to his lips and kissed it. He was so proud of her. She was amazing and she didn't even know it.

"I understand now though, why you want to kill Jordan, and I can't say I blame you."

"We won't kill him in cold blood, you don't have to worry about that," Zach spoke in a calm voice. "But I don't believe he'll come along nicely and go to the sheriff. He'll go down fighting."

"After his treatment of me, I believe you're right." Lily patted Jenny on the back and the baby burped. "I still don't know why he didn't kill me. I figure he was interrupted. Someone must have come into the store. It's the only thing I can think of. The distraction could even have been you Zach. He could've gone down the outside stairs while you came up the inside ones. That makes sense to me. From what you've said, I don't think he would have stopped for any other reason."

"To think I might have missed him by only seconds...that possibility pisses me off. I could have ended this." Zach wanted to hit something, preferably Jordan. A wall would do, but he controlled himself and pounded his fist into his hand.

"Maybe not," said Liam, who spoke in a reasonable tone. "He might have used Lily to escape, like he did with Ellie, just a couple of months ago. He might have hurt her worse than he did, just to get away. None of us want to see that happen again."

Zach stood. He couldn't sit still and paced back and forth in front of the fireplace. "I might know where to start. A bunch of food stands surround the laundry I use in Chinatown. And I know they rent the rooms above the laundry to whites. The owner of most of those businesses, Wu, is a good man. He'll tell us where Jordan has gone to ground."

"Please be careful." Lily gave Jenny back to Becky and rose. She went to Zach, wrapped her arms around his waist and held him.

He returned the embrace for several moments before pulling away. Then he decided he needed to hold her as much as she needed him, put his arm around her shoulders and pulled her close.

He raised her chin with his knuckle until she looked up at him. "I'll be careful. I have too much to live for to be careless." He lowered his lips to hers and kissed her thoroughly.

"Shall we go? I want to get this done so our families can be safe again," said Liam, who pulled the pistol from his belt and checked the load.

Zach and Jake performed the same action, making sure their weapons were fully loaded and ready to go. Running out of ammunition before the deed was done would do no one any good.

They left, making sure the ladies were well protected by the hired men. That didn't stop Zach from worrying. The incident with Jordan stabbing Ellie was fresh in his mind. Luckily, she'd recovered nicely and was now pregnant with her and Liam's first child together.

Thinking about new life when you're about to end another seemed apropos.

The brothers walked three-abreast through the town. Men moved out of their way when they saw the determination on their faces. Women scurried with their children, into nearby establishments and watched them pass through open doorways and windows. The atmosphere was as if Deadwood had been waiting for this showdown.

CHAPTER 14

Zach wanted this. He told Lily the truth when he said he thought Jordan would go down fighting. What he hadn't said was he would beat Jordan to within an inch of his life for having hurt Lily, if he gave up. He supposed he'd have to get in line behind his brothers for that privilege. But they wouldn't kill the murderer in cold blood, even if that was what he deserved.

They found Wu, a short Chinese man with a long braid down to his waist. He was directing the women who worked at the laundry on what kind of service his customers required. When he saw Zach come in, he broke into a wide smile. "Anderson. You come see Wu but no bring clothes." He frowned. "What you need from Wu? You not look happy for newly married man. Bullet wound pains you?"

"No, Wu, I'm fine. I need your help, though. I'm looking for a man. A white man, this height." He indicated a height level by bringing his hand up to his nose. "Sometimes he's bald and sometimes he has red hair and beard." Zach pointed to his hair and chin. "Have you seen him?"

Wu nodded. "Yes. He rent room four, up there." He pointed to the windows above the laundry.

"That room?" Excitement poured through Zach as he pointed at the open window. "The one that looks out over the street?"

Wu nodded again. "Yes, that room."

"Do you have a key? I don't want to break down the door."

"You no break door," insisted Wu with a shake of his head. "You break, you buy."

"Yes," agreed Zach, "I'll pay you for it, but I'd rather have a key."

Wu handed him a big skeleton key. "This work."

"Thank you. I'll give it back, shortly."

Zach held up the key for his brothers to see, turned and took the stairs inside the building two at a time, followed by Liam. Jake went around to the back of the building. Zach and Liam stood on either side of the door to Number Four, out of direct line of sight. Zach pushed open the door. When no shots were fired from within, he peeked around the corner of the door jamb into the room. Empty.

The room was simply furnished with a bed, cheap wood nightstand, table and single straight-backed chair. On the table lay the red wig and the rest of the red beard that Lily had torn off. An extra shirt hung on a peg on the wall to the right of the door. Nothing remained to indicate when Jordan had been here, but they knew not much time has passed since he'd beaten Lily and she'd ripped off his beard.

Zach looked out the window, scanned the area and realized Jordan could have seen them march up the street. "He saw us coming," he said to Liam." Let's check with Jake and see if he saw anything."

They went down the back stairs and found Jake standing at the bottom, gun drawn and in his hand, ready to go.

"We missed him," said Zach to Jake. "Let's go back to your house."

With long strides, Liam was already

moving back down the street. Zach and Jake fell into step behind him. All three of them were disappointed and silent on the trip back.

~*~

He ran between the stalls, keeping to the shadows as much as possible. That was close. If he hadn't looked up at that moment and peered out the window, he'd have been captured. He must have been careless. How did they find him?

Jordan hadn't planned on this but if he was one thing, that quality was resilient. What to do now but face the beast in its own lair? He knew Becky would be home. The house was safe. At least the Andersons' thought so. Feeling certain both of the women, maybe all three of them, would be at Jake's house, he headed in that direction.

He had no trouble recognizing the hired guns guarding the house. Two were at the front of the house, legs apart and arms folded across their chests. He'd check the back.

Only one man was here, though he was the size of the two men at the front put together. He watched for a couple of minutes, deciding the best approach, when he noticed the man grab his stomach, look both ways and then high tail it off the porch and toward the outhouse.

Jordan had no idea how or why he got so lucky but he would take advantage of the situation. He sprinted to the back porch, up the steps and into the house.

He came into the kitchen. A large, rectangular table dominated the room with twelve straight-backed chairs around it. Next to the matching hutch was the door he looked for, the one that led out into the rest of the house.

He slowly and quietly opened the door, peering into what appeared to be a hallway. Voices came from the right end of the hall, so he slipped out of the kitchen into the hall and made his way down to where the voices grew louder.

The hall opened into the living room. Two women, Lily and Becky, sat on the sofa. Becky, with her bright red hair, held a baby with the same shade of hair. He knew from his research the baby was a girl named Jenny. Anyone other than Lily would have faded into the background in the presence of such vibrancy, but not Lily. Her blond hair shone like gold.

He pulled his gun and walked into the

room.

"Good day, ladies."

Both women gave startled gasps but much to his surprise, neither screamed. That pleased him.

"You!" Lily, rose from the sofa, putting herself between him and Becky and Jenny.

"Lily. I'd hoped we'd spend more time together. Our last encounter was so rudely interrupted."

"You're insane, Jordan. You'll never get out of here alive."

He liked her defiance. She would be a treasure and killing her would be special. "But I will and I'm taking you with me."

"No, you're not," said Lily, standing with her legs akimbo and her hands on her hips. "I know what you did to Ellie and I'm not letting you do that to me."

"Then I'll do it to Becky and you'll come with me anyway."

Gaze narrowed, Lily stood her ground.

She really was magnificent. He hadn't seen anyone like her for a long time.

"I won't let you. You can shoot me, maybe even kill me, but you'll die. Two men are out front that will be in here at the first shot and you'll die in a hail of bullets like the scum you are."

"You'll never get off the first shot," growled Zach from behind Jordan, just as the front door slammed open and Jake and Liam entered the fray. "If you don't drop that gun now, I'll shoot you where you stand."

"I may shoot him anyway. It would be more of a chance than he gave Elizabeth," said Jake. His voice shook.

"Alright, alright. I'm dropping the gun." Jordan let the weapon fall from limp fingers.

"Now kick it away," ordered Zach.

With all the guns on him, he did as he was told and kicked it to the side.

"Lily, baby, go pick up the gun," instructed Zach.

She nodded and stepped toward the fallen weapon.

Jordan lunged forward, hoping to grab her and the revolver.

Shots rang out from behind and in front of him.

Lily screamed and dropped to the floor.

He felt the burning pain in his back first, just for a moment, then it was overshadowed by the pain in his chest, which brought him to his knees.

"You were warned," said Zach, standing over him, his gun still drawn. "You'll die now, just like Elizabeth did. Just like countless others have. No doctor, no friends. Only Satan to take away your evil soul."

"It wasn't supposed to happen this way," said Jordan, his voice sounded funny to his own ears. "You all were supposed to die, not me." He fell face first to the floor, his own blood strangling him.

Zach stepped over Jordan's body and helped Lily to her feet. "Are you all right? Are you hurt?" He ran his hands up and down her arms and over her back.

"I'm fine, just scared." She burst into tears and walked into Zach's waiting arms.

He'd never felt anything so wonderful as having Lily in his arms. Alive. "You don't know scared. When I came in here and saw him holding his gun on you, I couldn't breathe."

He hugged her tighter then took her head between his palms, lifted her chin until she stared upward with those beautiful blue eyes of hers. "Oh Lily, don't ever scare me like that again. I couldn't survive if anything happened to you." His hungry lips met hers. The kiss seared and rejuvenated. Reaffirmed their love for each other.

Zach turned to look at his brothers. Jake was holding Becky and Jenny. All three of them were crying, Jenny the loudest.

Liam stood, his hand on the door knob. "I'm getting the sheriff. I'll handle this. Zach, take Lily home. Jake, take Becky and Jenny upstairs."

"Thanks, Liam," said Jake, then he turned and led his family out of the room, away from the carnage.

"Yes, thanks, Liam." Relief flooded Zach. "The sheriff knows where to find me if he needs me." He grabbed Lily's hand. "He's probably got a wanted poster on Jordan. Tell him to keep the bounty. I don't want anything to do with it. I doubt you or Jake do either."

"That's the truth. I'm sure the sheriff can use it, too," said Liam, with a sharp nod. "Now get. Get home and love your wife."

"You don't have to tell me twice."

~*~

Lily couldn't get Zach home fast enough. Having nearly died, all she could think about was getting Zach inside her. She needed to feel alive, feel whole. Only Zach could give that to her. More than anything she wanted to make love with Zach.

She ran up the stairs to their apartment, Zach close behind her. As soon as she got inside the door, she began on her buttons, her hands flying over them. Then she pulled off her dress, stepped out of it and left it in a heap on the floor.

Zach grabbed her and swung her around in his arms. "Hold on there. We don't have to be in a hurry. We've got all the time in the world."

"You don't understand," she said, pulling back and tackling the hooks on her corset. "I don't want to wait. I want you in me. I want to feel your skin with mine. I need to know I'm alive." This last was a plea and she turned her back to him.

Zach came behind her. "I understand, sweetheart, and I'll make you feel more alive than ever, but slow down and enjoy."

"Next time. This time, fast. Now." She dropped her corset to the floor and took the binding from her breasts. Her hands came up and caressed her breasts and pinched the nipples. "Love me, Zach, love me."

His eyes lit up and Zach reached forward, tugged on the ribbon that held up her bloomers and watched as they followed the corset and the dress to the living room floor. Lily started to follow her clothes to the floor.

"No. Dammit. I won't take you like an animal on the floor." He grabbed her hand and dragged her to the sofa. "Lie down and wait while I get my clothes off."

She could hardly stand it. She played with her breasts and ran her hands over her stomach, down to her mons and pressed. God, the sensation. She thought she would die from the wanting.

Zach had his clothes off in record time and was there beside her.

"Hurry, Zach, I need you now." Smiling, she held her arms up toward him.

"You are a greedy little thing." He came down upon her and slid into her waiting warmth. Then he moved within her. Slowly.

"No," she pleaded, "fast, hurry. Love me, now."

"Shh," said Zach, tenderly kissing her lips. "I understand what you need, let me give it to you."

He understood all too well what she was

feeling. He felt it, too, though he didn't know what to call this yearning. This need to affirm life and loving and joy, after something terrible has happened. But he wanted her to slow down, enjoy, really feel, what they were doing and what they were to each other.

Lily was in a frenzy, her hands running up and down his back. She kissed him hard. Grazed his lips with her teeth.

He pulled back and slammed into her, giving her what she wanted. Again and again, until he was on the verge of losing himself. Then he reached between their straining bodies, and barely touched her.

She exploded.

"God, Zach," she screamed. "I love you."

The words were all he needed and he found his own paradise.

Slowly, both breathing hard, they clung together, limp from their exertions.

"I needed that," said Lily, nuzzling her nose against his damp neck. "I needed to have you with me, to have you spill your seed in me. I needed to feel life after all that happened today."

"I know. I did too. It's not easy to kill someone, even when you want to so bad it hurts. And I wanted to kill Jordan for what he did to you." He touched her bruised jaw and gently traced her swollen eye with his finger and his throat tightened. "I would have preferred to beat the crap out of him, like he did you, but he didn't give me the chance. God, Lily, I was so scared."

"Hush, now. We're here, we're unharmed, and have the rest of our lives ahead of us."

"I hope you get pregnant right away. I want a big family." He brushed a strand of hair from her forehead. "How about you?"

"I like children. Seeing Jenny, makes me want another baby. Gemma is growing up so fast. I don't know how many children I want. As many as the good Lord, sees fit to grant us, I guess."

He rolled off her and onto his feet, then held out his hand. "Come with me, Mrs. Anderson."

She took his hand and he led her to the bedroom. There, they made love many more times that day and night. Forgetting to eat, feasting on each other and the glow of their love.

The next morning, Zach surprised Lily with breakfast in bed.

"This is so nice of you. I feel exhausted." She grinned. "I don't think I got any sleep."

"Well don't expect to get any today." He sat on the edge of the bed next to her. "We're driving to Liam's to get Gemma. Now that it's safe, it's time we brought our daughter home."

"Oh, Zach, I love you more every day. There is nothing I want more than to bring Gemma home."

He leaned down and kissed her. "Thank you, Lily, for loving me. I waited a long time to find you."

She reached up and ran her hand along the stubble on his jaw. "I didn't think I could ever love anyone, especially a Yankee," she said, her voice dripping with her southern accent on the word 'Yankee'. "But you proved me wrong. You stayed with me and loved me when I gave you nothing back. I love you, Zach Anderson."

He kissed her, nuzzled her neck and kissed her again. "Eat, and then get dressed. Our family will be back together today. I bet Gemma is as ready to get home as we are to have her. She was ready to come back a few days ago."

"I know. You've given me this wonderful

breakfast, but I'm too excited to eat." She set the tray on the bed next to her and then stood. "I can hardly wait to see my baby girl."

Zach smiled. He loved seeing Lily happy. The sight was his joy in life. Anything he could do to that end he would do. Gemma was a big part of it, both Lily's happiness and his own. He loved that little girl just like she was his daughter and now, he guessed, she was.

He may have taken nearly forty years but it was worth the wait. His family was worth the wait.

"Ready?" asked Lily when she finished dressing.

"Ready. Let's go."

They walked down the stairs and then locked hands for the walk to Jakes to get the buckboard.

Zach had everything he could ask for and was filled with gratitude. A beautiful wife and daughter, a growing business and wonderful brothers. He'd finally found his life.

EPILOGUE

Zach sat with Lily and watched their children play tag in the front yard of their house, on the outskirts of Deadwood. They didn't work in the store anymore, instead had hired Mrs. Ferguson to manage it. Business was good, the mine was still producing and neither they nor their children would ever have to worry about money. Life was good.

Gemma, the oldest of his children, was sixteen now. Hard to believe he and Lily had been married more than ten years. And here she was, heavy with their sixth child. Adam, his eldest son, was ten and at the moment teased his little brother, Benjamin, seven. Ben was a gypsy, like Zach. He'd never seen it happen more than once in a generation but there it was. Liam's Hannah and his Ben both taking after his gypsy great-grandmother and himself—with their black hair and cobalt blue eyes.

Lily, knowing him so well she knew what he was thinking, said, "I told you I wanted a baby with your coloring when Ben was born. Somehow you always see that I get what I want."

Then they'd gotten a real surprise with Mary and Alice. Twins. Five now, they were the babies of the group until this new one came along. They looked just like their mother and sister, golden blond hair and cornflower blue eyes.

Adam was the fish out of water. He looked like Uncle Liam. Dark brown hair and gray eyes. But Zach didn't care what his children looked like or who they looked like, they were his and he loved them all.

"What variety of child do you think we'll get this time?" he asked Lily, who sat next to him on the porch swing. He rested his arm around her shoulders.Pleased that whenever they were relaxing together they had to be touching. *He* had to be touching. He still couldn't get enough of his beautiful wife.

"I don't know." She grimaced.

"Lily?"

"Yes," she said breathily, but with a wan smile.

"Are you in labor?"

"Umm, that is yes, dear."

"You've been in labor all morning, haven't you?" he admonished her.

"Well, yes, but the pains have only gotten bad just now. I guess you'd better help me into the house."

"Gemma," he shouted, standing and helping Lily to her feet.

"Yes, Daddy."

"Go get Doc Cochran, tell him—"

"I know. Mama's having a baby."

He grinned at his eldest daughter. "Yes, Mama's having a baby."

Gemma took off running and the other children gathered around Lily.

"Are you all right, Mama?" asked Alice fretfully. Alice was his little worrier. She worried about everything and everyone. The child would have stomach problems before she was an adult.

"Yes, Alice, Mama's fine. I just need to go upstairs now."

"Okay, look out," said Adam. "Daddy is gonna carry Mama upstairs."

"He can't do that," said Mary. "Mama's too big."

"Yes, he can, he always does when Mama has a baby. Just watch." Adam grinned.

Zach laughed, gathered Lily into his arms and carried his very pregnant wife upstairs to their bedroom.

A few minutes later, Gemma returned with the doctor.

"Good afternoon, Anderson children," Doc called on his way behind Gemma to the bedroom.

When he got there and saw Zach he said, "I don't suppose I'll get you to leave for this one either, will I, Zach?"

"Nope," said Zach with a wide smile. "I've been here for all my babies, except Gemma, and I won't change now."

"You know," said Doc, "that first time with Adam was a special occasion. I needed your help since I had a broken arm. Most fathers are not in the birthing room."

"Well, I'm not most fathers. I waited a long time to find my Lily." He rested his hand on Lily's bulging stomach. "I want my babies to know their father loves them and I love their mother too much to let her go through this alone."

"Will you both stop arguing, and someone catch this baby that is coming. Now!" shouted Lily.

Doc checked and sure enough the baby was coming.

The girl had dark, black hair and if she'd stop hollering long enough to open her eyes, Zach would bet they would mirror his own.

Doc cleaned her up, wrapped her in a blanket and handed her to Zach.

"Looks like we have us another gypsy, sweetheart," he said to Lily.

"And you told me they happened only once in a generation."

"And so they did until you." He bent and kissed her forehead. "You broke the pattern, Lily. You made your own luck, your own family. You broke all the rules. What shall we name her?"

"Abigail," said Lily, lifting her arms for the baby. "Let me have that sweet baby of mine. It's been too long since I've held a babe in my arms."

After brushing a kiss on her head, Zach

placed Abigail in her mother's arms.

Lily kissed the baby's head, counted her finger and her toes.

"The kids are dying to come in. Gemma has already peeked in twice."

"Let them inside, but in just a moment," said Lily. "I want to take some time for just the two of us with her."

Doc Cochran cleared his throat. "Everything looks great Lily, as usual. I'll tell the kids to come up in five minutes. Gemma should keep them corralled that much longer."

When they were alone, Zach leaned down and kissed Lily on the lips. "Thank you for making me the happiest man in the world. You seduced me the day I saw you and I've been enchanted ever since. Thank you for loving me, my sweet wife."

"Always, husband of mine. Always."

ABOUT THE AUTHOR

Cynthia Woolf is the award winning and best-selling author of eighteen historical western romance novels, one novella and one short story with more books on the way. She was born in Denver, Colorado and raised in the mountains west of Golden. She spent her early years running wild around the mountain side with her friends.

Their closest neighbor was one quarter of a mile away, so her little brother was her playmate and her best friend. That fierce friendship lasted until his death in 2006.

Cynthia was and is an avid reader. Her mother was a librarian and brought new books home each week. This is where young Cynthia first got the storytelling bug. She wrote her first story at the age of ten. A romance about a little boy she liked at the time.

Cynthia loves writing and reading romance. Her first western romance Tame A Wild Heart, was inspired by the story her mother told her of meeting Cynthia's father on a ranch in Creede, Colorado. Although Tame A Wild Heart takes place in Creede that is the only similarity between the stories. Her father was a cowboy not a bounty hunter and her mother was a nursemaid (called a nanny now) not the ranch owner.

Cynthia credits her wonderfully supportive husband Jim and the great friends she's made at CRW for saving her sanity and allowing her to explore her creativity.

TITLES AVAILABLE

GENEVIEVE, Bride of Nevada, American Mail-Order Brides, Book 36
THE HUNTER BRIDE, Hopes Crossing 1
GIDEON, The Surprise Brides
MAIL ORDER OUTLAW – Book 1 The Tombstone Brides
MAIL ORDER DOCTOR – Book 2, The Tombstone Brides
MAIL ORDER BARON – Book 3, The Tombstone Brides
NELLIE – The Brides of San Francisco 1
ANNIE – The Brides of San Francisco 2
CORA – The Brides of San Francisco 3
JAKE - Book 1, Destiny in Deadwood series
LIAM - Book 2, Destiny in Deadwood series
ZACH, Book 3, Destiny in Deadwood series
CAPITAL BRIDE (Book 1, Matchmaker & Co. series)
HEIRESS BRIDE (Book 2, Matchmaker & Co. series)
FIERY BRIDE (Book 3, Matchmaker & Co. series)
TAME A WILD HEART (Book 1, Tame series)
TAME A WILD WIND (Book 2, Tame series)
TAME A WILD BRIDE (Book 3, Tame series)
TAME A SUMMER HEART (short story, Tame series)
TAME A HONEYMOON HEART (short story, Tame series)

WEBSITE – www.cynthiawoolf.com

NEWSLETTER - http://bit.ly/1qBWhFQ